MW01075556

Because I Wanted You

BECAUSE I WANTED YOU

ANNIE GARRETT

ST. MARTIN'S PRESS ❈ NEW YORK

Grateful acknowledgment is given for permission to reprint the poem "Fame is a bee," by Emily Dickinson. From *The Complete Poems of Emily Dickinson*, edited by Thomas H. Johnson. Copyright 1929 by Martha Dickinson Bianchi, copyright © renewed 1957 by Mary L. Hampson. By permission of Little, Brown and Company (Inc.).

Design by Maureen Troy

Library of Congress Cataloging-in-Publication Data

Garrett, Annie
   Because I wanted you   /   by Annie Garrett. — 1st ed.
     p.   cm.
   ISBN 0-312-15427-5
   I. Title.
  PS3557.A71837B44   1997
  813'.54—dc21   97-5493
                                              CIP

First Edition: June 1997

10 9 8 7 6 5 4 3 2 1

For my friend,
who bought a one-way ticket

Fame is a bee,
It has a song—
It has a sting—
Ah, too, it has a wing.

—EMILY DICKINSON

Because I Wanted You

CHAPTER ONE

They had named her Ruby Blossom Bottom. Ruby because she was their jewel. Blossom after her great-grandmother. Bottom because it was her daddy's name and his daddy's before him and because there was no escaping it. There were days, and today was one of them, when she woke in the still, colorless part of the morning and believed she was waking on the mountain in Kentucky. Her legs were twisted and tight against her body. Her heartbeat raced at her temple and again low on her neck. She was hot and damp and ashamed of something she couldn't even name.

Rolling toward the window, she watched the rising sun cast color down the tree-lined valley of Fifth Avenue and filter into the penthouse apartment, where, she realized again, and with relief, she had escaped. She had. The man breathing on the other side of the vast mattress was proof. The garnets and the ambers of the old tapestries, the antiques from the best auction houses, they too were proof. And the Dutch timepiece . . . Oh, cripes, the time. She bolted out of bed and, as she passed the mirror on her dressing table, glimpsed herself in the silk nightgown, saw the red tousle of hair; there she was: Ruby Maxwell. Still Ruby Maxwell running late.

Joad would've been downstairs five minutes already. She pulled something Donna Karan and easy out of her closet, buttoned it even as she sat down at the dressing table. She put on her face without seeing it, traced the eyelids in kohl, sculpted the cheeks with powder blush. As a child she'd spent hours composing her expression in a little dime-store mirror she'd found on the school playground. She'd sucked in her cheeks and pretended the cheap little glass was a camera recording the way her pale skin stretched smooth over precipitous cheekbones. She'd narrowed her eyes and imagined the bright lights deepening the shadow under her square jaw and blanching out the freckles scattered across her nose. Hour after hour, she'd daydreamed that the camera was seeing her, nipping and tucking her into someone else, someone far, far away.

Her eyes darted again to the old Dutch clock on the mantel and then immediately back to the beveled mirror and her reflection. She traced on lipstick but didn't even have time to test it. No matter. All day, she would have to smile without always exactly meaning it. Why do it before her mascara was even dry?

Stepping into new suede Maud Frizon heels, she

glanced at the bed. Paul hadn't stirred. His breath moved evenly in and out, quiet as the ticking clock. She hesitated, then crossed hastily to the bed and bent over him, dashing a kiss on his right cheek, where he would find the lipstick impression when he went in to shave. It was the least she could give him, this daily souvenir of her affection.

Poor Paul, she thought, as she stepped into the elevator and pressed the lobby button three times fast. And it struck her, even as the words echoed in her—it struck her as ironic and absurd and unutterably sad that she should think that of Paul Carrigan. But there it was. *Poor Paul.*

She flashed her first smile of the day at the doorman, and it spread into the real thing as Joad held the limo door open for her. He bobbed on the balls of his feet, still the asphalt athlete, always moving, moving. "Mornin', RubyDoo," he said as he took her elbow and guided her into the leather interior. Folding his rubberband frame in behind the wheel, Joad bounced in the seat twice to settle his energy down, then handed her back a Starbucks cup. "Decaf skim mochaccino with cinnamon," he reported, but she had no doubt of it. He always bought an espresso for himself and a decaf for her.

"Bless your heart," she told him.

"Dag, Ruby," he said, as he studied her in the rearview mirror. "Who stepped on your face?"

"What?" she said, angling past him for a shot at the mirror. She couldn't see any egregious mascara smears or blush smudges. "What?"

"Under your eyes, woman. Look at those bruises."

She grimaced. "Hush up and drive. I'm just a little tired."

He grimaced right back, fired the engine. When he had nosed the Mercedes into the bumper-car traffic, he picked up his copy of *Variety* and waved it. "Great ratings this week," he told her. "Wanna see?"

"I'll take your word for it."

"Top of the charts." Joad read the trades the way a lot of guys read Yankees scores or the Intel index.

"I believe you."

"Dag, Ruby."

He tapped the wheel to some music that was playing in his head, something hip-hop. He'd been doing that the first time she met him, when they were both working on the Spencer campaign. He'd introduced himself as Joad Finkelstein, and of course she'd heard of his dad, a famous-among-the-intelligentsia Communist essayist from *The Nation* who was married to an NYU lit teacher, all of which accounted for the *Grapes of Wrath* nomenclature. Anyway, Joad had of course gone public schools all the way, and about the time he hit Bronx Science, he started acting like a brother, like his homies. And Ruby had to admit that despite blue eyes and curls the color of halvah, the guy did have soul. He also had one of the quickest minds she'd ever met and one huge failing: He was afraid of his own potential. When she'd been tapping talent for the show, she'd wanted him onboard. "I'm working on my screenplay," he'd demurred. Since it was the same screenplay he'd been working on ever since she'd known him, and as far as she knew he'd never told anyone what it was about or even what genre it was, she pressed. Finally, he said he'd work for her if he could be her driver; that way he could write on the side, and anyway, he'd done a thesis on limo drivers at Princeton and had always thought it a romantic line of work. She told him not to be ridiculous and reminded him that he didn't even have a driver's license, and he'd shrugged and said he'd get one. And he had. Now, he dug the heel of his hand into the horn, and she thought how easily he'd nailed the nuances of city driving.

She looked out the window at all the kids in private-school uniforms and the men in suits and the women in skirts and sneakers rushing toward the Eighty-sixth Street subway station. She remembered what that felt like—to take the steps down at a staccato pace and hip your way through the turnstile while not spilling your coffee and race onto the train just before the door closed and to bump into some guy just hard enough so that a little coffee spurted up out of the drinkhole and all over his yellow tie and then to apologize all over yourself and then have to stand there crushed up next to him for six stops because it was rush hour and everybody was going your way. It wasn't so bad, really, looking back.

"You gonna watch the TV today?" Joad asked over his shoulder.

"Nah." She reclined, rested her head on the high back of the seat. She knew full well, and naggingly, that she should be sharpening herself against the morning shows, but not yet. "Give me some music," she said.

Joad's index finger hovered over the CD changer's buttons. "Salt-N-Pepa, maybe?"

"You wish," she said.

"Boyz II Men?" He tweaked an eyebrow at her hopefully.

"Bryan Ferry," she said.

He groaned, and she knew he was just full of crap because she'd once had the guys from Chic on her show and even they had found Bryan Ferry inspirational.

She aimed a mollifying grin at Joad's rearview mirror. Then, she took off her shoes, which pinched, and put her feet up in the seat that faced her. Music rose around her like incense, and she tried to disappear into its tantalizing tones, tried to follow Ferry's eerie voice, beckoning. It was night music, haunted by shadows and lights in the distance. It had always meant Manhattan to her, Manhattan as Oz. She had first heard Bryan Ferry the night she found Paul, or the night Paul had found her. And that seemed a long time ago: seven years ago this very night.

At seventeen, she had run away with her cousin Liza. They had met just after dawn in Jackson at the bus station, paid their Dairy Queen countergirl money for two tickets to New York. Liza had her own reasons and a suitcase full of L'eggs panty hose and polyester blouses from the Goodwill shop, all of which she dressed up with her grandma's old jewelry. Ruby had her ACT scores and her 4.0 grade-point average and a letter of recommendation from a teacher named Dewey.

None of the kids called him Mr. anything. He was too young and spirited to be anything but Dewey to them. The boys liked him because he could target you with the football from forty yards, and the girls because he had a wiry shock of hair, black-and-blue as a crow's wing, and also odd, grape-colored eyes. Ruby liked him especially because he could quote Shakespeare and make her hear how it echoed with familiar things. He made her understand that no matter how President Johnson and Walker Evans and Al Capp had portrayed the mountain people in their poverty, something of Shakespeare's voice survived through them. Dewey believed that. He was a graduate student from Eastern Kentucky, who'd had a chance to make it out of Appalachia but instead had come back to try and make a difference. To Ruby, he had made all the difference.

He had taken her walking that first spring up on Rain Crow Mountain, and she had made him laugh with stories about what it was like over on Shoulderblade, over at her family's cabin perched precariously above the hollow, where, when the wind wasn't blowing through the pines, you could hear the creek rattle past. It was her habit to spin her own hardships into a story the way the women of her family had long ago spun flax from the garden into cloth for their kids' backs. You made do with what you had. And making it all into a story was the best she could do, telling it like gossip, like gossip that hurt somebody else and not Ruby herself and all her brothers. "We had this old hen we called Easter because she always hid her eggs," she told him, laughing. "Sometimes our only chance at breakfast was finding whether she'd laid 'em in the seat of the broken-down tractor Dad never hauled away or in Raphy's boot by the back door or in the hollow stump down where the sweet williams grow."

The mountain path they were following was more like a tunnel through the heavy growth of rhododendrons. No sunlight penetrated, but the mountain laurel was blooming and the pines scented the air. She thought how the green was like a room around them, hushed as a church. Somewhere during her storytelling, Dewey had sat down on a boulder that poked up out of a coldwater stream, and she had settled on another. They had put their bare feet in a quiet pool, moved their soles over the stones rubbed to velvet by the spring torrents. Then his foot had touched hers. The cold water had numbed her to most everything, but she thought she felt it and then confirmed it with a glance. They stayed that way for a while, his foot over hers.

That's how it had started. And it had ended with Ruby and Liza on a Greyhound. They had come to Manhattan, but they couldn't find any place they could afford to live, not there or in Brooklyn or in Queens. The only apartment they found was in the South Bronx, in a lone building standing on a block of others that looked as though they

had been bombed. Even theirs had elevator shafts gaping
open and falling-apart stairs. Down on the street, the two
girls stood out as much as their building: their translucent
Scot-Irish skin, their musical drawls, Ruby with her lean
and towering build topped by the red hair, Liza with her
blond fall that swished back and forth across her belt. All
these marked them as strangers.

For the first few days, they came and went to the subway stop together. They walked fast for the first block, faster on the second, and broke full-tilt into running on the
third. Nobody moved to harm them, but guys whistled and
called lewd things to them, chided them for not smiling at
the suggestions. And one day, Ruby had just pulled herself
up and faced down a short guy whose quicksilver tongue
especially impressed his towering buddies. "Excuse me,"
she said. "We haven't met. My name is Ruby." She held
out her hand.

He glared at her a minute, then a grin spread across
his face like wind blowing across a still pond. And she
grinned back. He introduced himself as Bone, and after
that, he always walked the full way with Ruby or Liza when
he saw one or the other headed to or from the subway. The
other guys held their tongues, and the ones who smiled at
Ruby, she smiled back.

Ruby made the trip to the subway every weekday, going
to Barnard and begging her case. She wrote letters. She
trailed the dean along the intersecting paths on the campus.
She introduced herself to anyone who would listen, tracked

down important alumni, the chairmen of scholarship committees. "Hey," she'd say. "I'm Ruby Blossom Bottom." She wrote it on every form she could find, signed it with the gravity that depended on somebody else seeing in it what she saw in herself: Ruby Blossom Bottom.

*J*oad turned up the music as he crossed the Queensboro Bridge. He was weaving around to its rhythms in spite of himself, although its power was somehow lost on Ruby today. Bryan Ferry's voice swirled emptily outside of her just as the sunlight swirled, sparkling, in the East River. As the car neared the far shore, they were greeted as usual by the billboard touting Ruby's talk show. Emblazoned with her face, it beamed down over the interborough traffic, her smile the size of a stretch limo. Ruby never looked at that billboard, and she didn't now.

She screwed her feet back into the suede pumps as Joad swung into the studio lot, through security, and under the awning that said only RUBY! Guilt nipped at her; she should've been using the drive time to return a few calls or at least to watch a taped snippet of what the other talk shows had done yesterday. But she hadn't. And all she could do now was draw a deep breath, steel herself, dab at her lipstick.

There were already a few fans waiting, only the professionals at this hour. Theirs were the faces she had started seeing again and again in the months since the show had rolled out in syndication. They had jobs in the lot's cafeteria or in maintenance, and they came every day or so to get her photograph signed for this friend or that. So they said. Maybe they sold them or hoarded them for a day when they might really be worth selling.

Anyway, when Joad opened the door for her, the autograph seekers pounced. Today they were all holding out the fresh issue of *Cosmo* with Ruby on the cover. She paused to sign some of them. *Ruby*, she wrote in sweeping letters engineered to leave no doubt how she saw herself and how she knew everyone else saw her too: *Ruby, Ruby, Ruby.*

*I*nside the atrium, her high heels sparked on the tile corridor and her stomach rumbled with the dread that was as familiar to her now as hunger. As always, the security guards nodded respectfully from their posts. The cleaning man paused in emptying the ashcan and grinned up at her. And when she emerged through the double glass doors into the office mazework of the show and her presence fell across the staffers working there, every face turned like a sunflower to her. Every one of them smiled.

"Morning," she trilled.

"Morning, Ruby," they chorused.

And then she closed her office suite's door behind her, wrenched off her shoes, exhaled. The blinds had all been drawn open, and there was a sesame bagel on her desk, tofu cream cheese on the side. Her personal assistant, Eden, was efficient that way, thought morning light would prevent a dip in the biorhythms and that breakfast was definitely not a cup of Starbucks on the way into work. Ruby could hear her in the adjoining office, already policing the blockade between Ruby and the riot of her responsibilities. The buzzing and knocking and ringing had begun, insistent: All those smiles had come calling.

Spreading a smear of tofu on a quarter of the bagel, Ruby was pierced for the umpteenth time with the question of what to do about Eden. Her assistant had been home-schooled among the northern California redwoods, the only child (overpopulation mathematics applied) of leftover-hippie parents who envisioned her following in their Birkenstock footsteps. Instead, Eden had put herself through college by being Cinderella at Disneyland and had graduated first in her class at UC–Santa Barbara. Afterward, though she wore her hair trimmed short like Louise Brooks and checked off her daily appointments 7 A.M. to 9 P.M. in a Filofax, she had suffered in Hollywood from the lack of family connections—no Spelling in her name, no Barrymore in her blood, no Tarsis offering a hand from a higher echelon in the Industry. So she moved East and applied to Ruby. She had accepted the job of personal assistant gamely but only with the understanding that within the first year Ruby would reward extra effort with promotion.

Ruby should never have agreed to such a thing. What you wanted was an assistant who was making an investment in you, who wanted to make your well-being their career.

But of course she had seen something of herself in the girl who had been forced to grab the rungs of the ladder and pull herself up. And Ruby had then and still did fully intend to reward her assistant. The only problem was that in those fleet twelve months, Eden had proved herself to be indispensable: Not only could she ably choreograph Ruby's harried schedule—and her whims—while remaining pacific as the ocean she was raised near, she also could summon a bitchiness that perfectly suited Ruby's needs. Somehow, sweetness had become Ruby's defining characteristic. She had been cast as America's favorite sister because she was a rarity: a real person on daytime television. She hugged her guests and called them honey. She blessed their hearts and cried with them. She actually said nice things that weren't encrusted with irony or encoded with skepticism. *TV Guide* had just hailed her as Merv reborn, a saint sent to save talk-show television from itself. Her publicity people had insisted she honor the magazine's request that she wear angel wings and a halo for the cover shoot. And if her own inborn sinew was going to be shackled into wings, she found it comforting to have someone loyal around who could wield a pitchfork.

Ruby felt oddly vulnerable, being famous. Everybody else in the world (or so it seemed) knew who she was, and most of them she didn't know from J. D. Salinger. Some celebrities enjoyed that sensation, she realized, and it *was* a sensation, being brushed with so many strangers' eyes. You could virtually feel it, a stroking. It could raise the fine hair on your arms. It could trickle down your spine like desire. An actress acquaintance of Ruby's had recently captivated a dinner party in Soho by describing what it felt like to be "face famous." Most of the people there that night were producers and agents and fashion designers, who were known by their names if not their faces, and they listened raptly as the blond actress with ridged cheekbones and hollowed cheeks described hitting it big opposite Tom Cruise in last summer's blockbuster: Before that, the actress said, she had walked around New York City feeling people's eyes pass through her as though she were Casper the Ghost. But now, "Every walk is like the Macy's Thanksgiving Day parade . . . and I'm the balloons." *Pop!* Ruby had said to herself. And as the starlet had gleefully laughed at her metaphor, and as the others, finding her irresistible, had joined in, Ruby had amused herself by imagining the actress deflating, hissing air and caving in on herself—just the way Kermit had the Thanksgiving he got stabbed by a streetlight on his way down Central Park West.

Ruby didn't trust fame. Sure, it was nice to be the first on any plane. It was nice to know you would never again have to crowd onto a subway train where St. Patty's Day revelers turned as green as their hats and urped on your new suede shoes (which had happened to her on the downtown D). It was nice to command respect, especially from powerful men who hired the cutest young Ivy League things for their offices and called them hon and asked them to stay late and drink Absolut. That was very nice, hearing those same men call you Ms. Maxwell. But . . .

God, wouldn't the girl she had been have kicked the butt of the woman she had become, complaining about how good she had it? But Ruby couldn't help herself. She knew now that celebrity wasn't what she had been looking for when she was nine years old, lying on the cool linoleum floor of the Zachariah County storefront library. Back then she had looked up exactly where her name would fall in the Funk & Wagnalls encyclopedia—right between Botticelli and Bottrop. Sitting there with her chewed fingernail on that little sliver of white page, she had felt swollen with potential. When her name was *right here*, wouldn't she be able to make everything the way it should be? Wouldn't her dad lose his power when she had hers?

Only now was she finding out what it cost to find your own power: Fame circumscribed your life. It put you in the barb-wire fence of other people's expectations. It bound you on somebody else's leash. In some ways, it had made her more vulnerable than she had been back at Shoulderblade. *Entertainment Weekly* might count her as one of the top-ten most powerful people in show business, but she didn't feel it as her power anymore. True, she'd gotten this far under whatever it was she had inside her. But now, it had somehow twisted on her: She felt her fame as a power *over* her. She needed other people—needed someone to wrangle the incessant phone calls and someone else to ensure that her hair wasn't betraying her, and she needed a whole team of writers to make her appear effortlessly sincere, and she couldn't get by anymore without one guy to manage her money and another her image and another her physique. She needed all those someones to hide behind on the little things because when it came to the big things there was no one but Ruby herself out there in the bright, unforgiving lights, out there casting the longest shadow around. It was as though her life were fenced onto a vast sun-bleached plain, and there were only a few trees under which she could find some shade from the sun, behind which she could hide from all the watching eyes for even the briefest respite. Chief among the trees in her life was Eden.

And as usual, Eden made sure Ruby had a minute to scan the front page of the *Times*, Page Six in the *Post*, and her horoscope in the *Daily News*, which Ruby didn't believe in any more than she believed in fortune cookies, but which she nevertheless always read because sometimes it felt good to get one that said what you wanted to believe. She still had a fortune in her pocketbook that had come with cold sesame noodles on a rainy night. It said, "Love never does wrong that can't be made right." She wanted to believe that.

Today's horoscope was boring, though, only a cautionary business-dealings kind of thing. Eden appeared as she read it, offered her apologies that it wasn't livelier, then doled out her spiel: Ruby's contract-renegotiation team needed her attention yesterday. Her accountant wanted her to sign off on her taxes. And her publicist required her nod on a couple of inquiries. There was a hesitation at the end of the list; Eden flushed, and Ruby knew instantly that her assistant wanted to schedule her own five minutes to broach her promotion. But the question went unasked, and though it hung perceptibly between them, Ruby left it unanswered.

A buzzer sounded in Eden's office.

"That'll be Fritz," Eden interpreted. "It's that time."

"That I can handle," Ruby said, standing up.

"What should I tell everyone else?" Eden asked. Ruby knew she was really saying, *What about me?*

Ruby sighed. "You'll think of something, hon. You always do."

Eden looked at her, opened her mouth, closed it, then turned to go.

"Edie?" Ruby called after her.

Eden turned expectantly.

Ruby really did want to come out and just say that she knew her deadline was up six days ago and that she did intend to do the right thing by Eden and sooner rather than later, but instead, she deflected: "What size shoe do you wear?" she asked.

Eden's expectant expression slid down into a smirk. "Eight," she said. "Big feet travel on my mom's side, peasant blood."

Ruby laughed. "These Mauds are supposed to be seven and a half to fit my seven-and-a-half feet. But they're torturing me. Could you maybe wear them for a while and see if you can stretch them out a little?" She held them out to Eden, as she continued: "I wouldn't ask but I bought them to go with the Vera Wang for that Met wingding next week, and how am I supposed to get through the night if I don't have any blood in my toes?"

Eden took the shoes.

"If you don't mind," Ruby added.

"This gives a new spin to the meaning of *personal* assistant," Eden said, stepping out of her own Loehman's specials and into the expensive high-heeled pumps. She swayed unsteadily.

"No wonder you made such a good Cinderella," Ruby teased.

"No wonder," Eden quipped as she picked up her discarded shoes.

"Thanks, sweetie," Ruby called after her, then she padded next door into her dressing room and paused in front of the triptych mirror. She'd always been narrow; brittle-thin, her mother called it. Her personal trainer liked to take credit for it, but lately it seemed her angularity was ground on an edge that had nothing to do with Nautilus or Stairmaster. Lately, she'd gone all sharp.

She climbed into the chair and really looked at her face for the first time that day. It was pathetic that she had to put on makeup just to ride into work and to read the papers and to eat one quarter of a bagel. She knew it. But she had been this way so long that she couldn't hope to change, not now when the pressure on how she looked and laughed and acted was so great. Years ago, her mama had demonstrated how to paint on Maybelline, saying, "You can be anybody you want to be." And of course Ruby had wanted to be *any*body else. So from junior high on, she had carried lipstick in her jeans pocket and reapplied it immediately after eating anything. She had redone her nails daily, finger and toe. She had darted into the girls' room and touched up her blush between class bells. It was vain, but it was a desperate vanity: It was her only hope. She remembered when Dewey had finally realized that. He had said softly, so softly, "Oh, Ruby, don't put all that pressure on your pretty face. Rely on what's in your head. Really." Still, all these years later, she couldn't even ride into work without cowering behind Erno Laszlo powders. Though it was plain, sitting here, that Joad was right: The Bergdorf Goodman makeup didn't hide anything, not the tense creases at the corner of her mouth, not the bruises of exhaustion the nightmare had left under both eyes. It didn't hide the old shame in her eyes. It didn't hide the pressure.

Fritz would manage magic, though; he notoriously did. He would recast her hair and buff her face down to the fresh skin and build it up again to suit the cameras. He would hide what she couldn't bear for the world to see.

"Morning, Glory," he sang now as he entered, lean Fritz with his late-Elvis haircut and his eyewear collection (which yesterday had numbered 206 pairs of glasses and four pairs of colored contact lenses).

"Morning, Fritzie," she answered, glad for the water running and then the blow dryer droning as she tried not to hear the echo that was called up from those words: *Morning, Glory.* Sometimes when he greeted her that way, it didn't send the electricity through her. Sometimes she didn't remember the other voice whispering those words to her a long time ago, didn't remember the way it had bound her with its soft cords. Not today, though. Today, she heard the echo, heard too the sound of the stranded birds in the morning dusk, and her big-boned brothers tossing themselves over in their bunks, and the wailing. She remembered those other hands in her hair, couldn't forget.

CHAPTER TWO

*A*fter exactly five people had nudged Ruby along the corridor by reporting the exact second of countdown to showtime, Eden handed off the customary liter of Evian and Ruby turned toward the soundstage. She took a swig of the water as she walked, left a lipstick smudge on the plastic bottle, and then had to submit to letting Fritz touch up the water damage to her makeup. "You always go and schmutz yourself," he chided her, even as her producer, His Own Self, known on the opening credits as Trev Jones, held the door for her and checked his watch again.

She smiled at him on the way through, which was more than he deserved, since he'd once again done it to her, meaning that once again she'd have to do it to him. The Muckety-Mucks in their high-concept-and-bottom-line wisdom had shackled her with him just when she needed him least. Lately, she spent more time undoing his work than doing her own. And people wondered why she felt she had to put in a full day, not disappearing after the show like some other talk show hosts she knew: damage control.

"Five minutes," Trev reminded her. It sounded like an accusation and was. She had been the one who insisted on the live format. He had fought to change it when he came aboard—and lost. Since then, he had let it be known loudly and often that it had given him more than his share of Maalox moments. But it was her show after all, and she thrived on the moment quivering irrevocably in the air. It was like old-time radio, early television. It was like life.

At first the audience didn't know she was there. Against their expectations, she had come from the same door they had, not from backstage. She swung a look over the whispering crowd. They always whispered at first, awed even as they realized how small the set was compared with how it looked from home when the theme music rolled after the Bounce commercial at ten in the morning every weekday. She stepped down the first few aisles and heard recognition murmur first in one corner and then spread across the auditorium like the sound of treetop birds at dawn: They saw her.

Her whole Madison Avenue–perfect demographic was represented. Not only the carefully accessorized moms from the outer boroughs and the Midwestern tourists off buses were here, but also the young corporate Dilberts stealing an hour out of the office and the Upper West Side professionals on maternity leave from Morgan Stanley. The ones nearest the aisle reached out their hands to her, and she took what ones she could. In the beginning, she had wanted to give each of them what they were looking for in her. She had looked them all in the eye and tried to say the thing they needed her to say. But she'd been at it so long now, so many shows following on so many shows, that their faces blurred. Sometimes at night, she lay in bed and tried to conjure up one face from her audience, one set of features she would recognize if she were to get on the M104 uptown and happen to sit next to that person. She couldn't do it. Not one. Ever.

The way she was tarrying with the guests was driving His Own Self to fidget. He had his headphones around his neck already, and he kept his wrist cocked so his watch was always facing him. Just to make his stomach churn, she stopped to autograph a HAPPY BIRTHDAY, MILTIE sign that three NYU kids hoped to hold up when the camera panned in their direction. Trev hitched up his pants. Poor Trev, he had the pedigree, if nothing else, to recommend him: He'd done time at Letterman and Oprah, had throttled Ricki through the first year. (Of course he hadn't lasted a week with Rosie, which was all Ruby had needed to know to confirm her own suspicions.) The Muckety-Mucks had paid dearly to woo him over to *RUBY!* but it was an investment they felt they couldn't pass up. Ruby's show had sprouted on Lifetime three years ago. As a live interviewer, Ruby had an absolutely fresh approach, according to the critics (even Jeff Jarvis). The cable audience couldn't get enough of her, especially if she was doing one of her retro episodes in which, say, she giggled with Mary Tyler Moore about the Powers That Were not wanting Laura Petrie to wear slacks, especially slacks that "cupped" too much. But no chances were to be taken with the *RUBY!* rollout to syndication. The Muckety-Mucks wanted to guard against what one of them called "Kathie Lee syndrome." They wanted to keep the teeth in Ruby's smile. In short, they wanted a good man behind their woman. The network unveiling, which introduced a more issue-oriented format, had been a brilliant ratings grabber, and as it approached the end of its first season, *RUBY!* was changing the country's morning-television landscape. The Muckety-Mucks, of course, couldn't praise Trev enough.

Barbed by that indignity, Ruby tried often to remind herself that maybe half what she got paid—half of that unbelievably huge, never-would've-dreamed-it salary—was solely for putting up with His Own Self. He was wormy. He had this lop of hair that hung over his eyes, a great convenience because he could not hold eye contact. Worse yet, he'd grown up pampered, hadn't hit a snag from Dalton to Yale. And he was no more than a boy (even though there was only a six-month difference in their ages): His jeans still puckered adolescently over his paltry little bum. Worst of all, and for this she just couldn't forgive him, was that he was a television terrorist who tossed around condescensions like "lowest common denominator" even as he doused everything with flammable sensationalism. He liked mindless conflagrations. Which was precisely *not* what had propelled her success.

Trev came up a few steps and took her arm, ushering her the rest of the way and installing her on the funky but comfortable set. The audience cheered. Taking her bow, she beamed at them. Then, turning to Trev, she did it to him once again. She changed the show—just as the clock over the control booth ticked off its final seconds. At his behest, she'd been in the Green Room earlier (something she'd never done before his time), and lucky thing, because he had a bunch of would-be guests in there that just didn't seem right to her. She didn't get any emotion off them. One was eating Tostitos out of a torn bag, all blasé. Another was double-checking his nosehairs in the mirror over the Mr. Coffee. Those two could stay put. She'd take one— the boy who wore hot-rod Doc Martens on his pigeon-toed feet, the one with the orange buzz cut and the sad amber eyes.

"What am I supposed to do with the others?" Trev protested in a razorlike whisper.

She shrugged. "Send them out to play hoops with Joad. They'll have a blast." The tic at the corner of Trev's right eye registered his fury, but, too bad, he was out of time. She saw him check his shirt pocket for a Maalox tab, even as he turned to take his place in the booth in front of the audience. There was nothing he could do now. It was her stage.

Ruby picked up the microphone. The lights came up. The crew adjusted the booms and the spots. The cameras whirred, zoomed in and out, got ready to go red light. Everyone focused on Ruby, waited on her, watched. It was as though she were in the center ring, just as she had wished when she was maybe five, and her brothers had sneaked her into the circus that came to town. Three rings had filled the patched tent, and at first she had wondered how she was going to divide her attention, how she was going to see everything there was to see, missing neither the girls in pink glitter on the high wire nor the clowns spilling out of bumper cars nor the chains of swaggering elephants. But then the man in the top hat and tuxedo tails moved into the spotlight and spoke with such grace and poise, and even when the light splintered into three beams, Ruby kept watching him as he strolled about on the fringes, holding the whole thing up with the rope of his fine voice, spinning it this way and that with nothing but supple inflection. After that, she wanted to be the guy in the top hat. Ruby wanted to be the one to tell the story. Because it seemed to her that the one who told the story did the magic. The one who told the story made everyone else move, pulled all the strings. Without the master of ceremonies and his beautiful words, the circus tent smelled like elephant dung, and the high-wire girls had runs in their stockings, and the clowns were just sad men who hadn't shaved in a while. That's all.

But Ruby hadn't expected telling the story to do what it had: It changed everything. And it had been nothing but an accident of timing, a fluke. She'd been volunteering on what turned out to be her last campaign, this one a gubernatorial bid. Mostly, she was into the hurly-burly of headquarters, which reminded her of her brothers somehow. She liked eating microwave popcorn out of a coffee filter and drinking coffee until three in the morning and then drinking Diet Pepsi for breakfast. She loved being part of a family of cocky little fighters from Brooklyn and eggheads from Riverside Drive and ambitious transplants from the suburbs. She spent more time with them than she did at home with Paul. The Candidate himself was relevant, certainly, but she knew why she was devoting so much of her time to him. And it wasn't because he would make the best leader ever. In fact, he hadn't been shy about living before he decided to become a politician, and so he was a huge target for controversy, the man who would be governor. As Election Day ticked closer, flu hit his headquarters simultaneously with a low blow from his opponent's campaign: The Candidate was accused of having dallied at Plato's Retreat as a young man. His much-vaunted spin master, a guy from Central Park West named Goldstein, was green and queasy with Spanish-something flu. They couldn't risk him on camera. And the Candidate himself naturally had to hover above this particular debate. So they had had no choice but to send Ruby. She had shaken all over. Her palms had wept. She hadn't been able to feel her knee joints. But when the camera clicked on, she shimmered. There she was with her sweet Southern-girl looks, her heavily lashed green eyes and her dimpled smile. The Republican's operative was disarmed. When he tiptoed over to the topic of homosexual encounters in Greenwich Village, Ruby looked straight at him and said, "What does it matter who he's screwing as long as it's not the taxpayers?" Then she blushed. Show stopped. Headlines made. Controversy upstaged.

After that, armed with what one newspaper columnist called her "straight-shot wit," she could get on the talk shows with her big red hair and her honey drawl and hit politically sensitive bull's-eyes with one arrow after another. She clipped off sound bites with her white teeth gleaming, sieving them through that smile: made for television. After the campaign, the candidate went to live in the governor's mansion in Albany. And she went to cable television, then to producers whose logo had been all over the Saturday morning cartoons, which made them even more cool to her, and from there to national television, where she was standing even now with the red light signaling they'd gone to living air, and she could feel it coming on, could feel the strange calm beginning to move into her blood like whiskey on a cold night, that strange calm distilled by the key lights, concentrated by the camera, everything drawn down and focused on this one moment in this one circle of light. Nothing else mattered. Everything else was suspended. The lights were up and blazing and the camera was moving in close. There was no past, no future: only now.

And now contained a boy and his mother and some

things they didn't want to admit to themselves or each other. She sat there with the boy first. At eighteen, he was old enough to think of himself as a man, yet young enough still to be rooted in his childhood: He told her how he'd been the best kid ever, how he'd had his own baby-sitting service, how he'd scored solid *B*-pluses, and how it had all changed when he said grace aloud at the Thanksgiving table and thanked the Lord for giving him parents who would understand when he told them he was gay.

Ruby let the silence stretch a moment, then asked, "And what did they say?"

The boy looked at his hands. "My father said, 'Please pass the mashed potatoes.'"

Ruby coaxed him through the rest of the story, which included his parents turning on the house alarm, changing the locks, and leaving him a note that used the word *faggot*. Which included him living on the street and getting into cars with old men who were so sick they needed respirators to breathe but who still knew how to use their wallet to get what they wanted. Which included getting an AIDS test and with it, the worst possible news.

Ruby cried when he got to that part. She couldn't help herself. But even as she wiped her eyes, she was aware of her critics judging her (which was the trouble with reading about yourself in the newspaper all the time). Either her tears were genuine spontaneity or they were pure disingenuous savvy. The sad thing was, it didn't really matter which. Not as long as she sold boxes of re-engineered tampons and bottles of European water and jeans cut for real women.

After a station break, Ruby came back alone with the mother, who confided that her boy had been a child as "sweet as August corn." She said: "When he was little, he'd bring me home flowers every day. He was picking the neighbors' daffodils and their peonies and their iris. We had the hardest time getting him broke of that. He was harder than a deer on those gardens." She smiled and laughed, but the sadness didn't leave her eyes. She was Catholic and truly believed that her son was sinning. "When he was a little boy, I used to think he was put on this earth to make me happy," she said wistfully. "I really did."

Ruby gave the cue for Trev to bring the boy back out. It was a horrible moment. When he walked out onto the stage in his fuchsia Doc Martens, the mother's face went white. The boy's went green, clashing with his hair. His eyes showed his vulnerability, and he kept himself turned toward Ruby like a plant reaching for the light. It was clear that of the two women sharing the stage with him, one had the power to devastate him, even if the other had the power of the camera.

Ruby held them both up, carried them. Her voice was hushed and comforting. She didn't cartwheel or back-flip or trigger Trev's fireworks. She merely told them their own story, repeated to them both what each had said. She held them together with nothing but the timbre of her voice, the thread of her narrative.

Finally, she asked the woman, "When you look at him, don't you see the same boy who picked you all those flowers?"

The woman's head shook side to side, not even glancing at her son.

Ruby looked at the boy, nodded her head in subtle encouragement. He cleared his throat. "It's just me, Ma," he said, his voice cracking like an adolescent's. "It's just who I am."

Ruby let the moment stretch between them and vibrate as though it were a wind harp with the tension blowing through it, gently, gently. "I know, honey," the mother said finally. "I've always known. Don't you think I've always known?" Tears streamed down her face. Her son batted at his own eyes with a fist, then reached for his mother's hand. She hesitated a moment, then curled her fingers around his.

Ruby might not even have been there, nor any of the hundred or so others gathered there in Studio 4B. She practically whispered her good-bye, seemingly serene and reverent in the moment, that one last, hushed moment when the camera watched intently and the audience sat holding its breath and the lights burned and when, as usual, she felt the emptiness low in her stomach, where she most hated herself for doing what she did and for getting paid so awful much to do it.

Chapter Three

The scent accosted her as she opened her office door. Ruby got ambushed by what she should've been expecting: seven overflowing bunches of lilacs. Eden had arranged them all around the room. There were antique whites and traditional lavender and that deep regal purple Ruby loved especially. In the corner of the wraparound windows was a tiny bouquet of the rare copper-colored ones that seized her heart. She crossed the room, touched the petals.

Ruby never knew where Paul found them in such variety. Maybe he had some arrangement with one of his family's friends—Martha Stewart or some other rich horticulturist with an embarrassment of blooms. Early on in their relationship, he had noticed how Ruby was drawn to the sidewalk display in front of a Korean market, where among the apricots and lemons and tulips there was a heady bunch of lilacs. She had run her fingers over the buds and breathed in the perfume, and that year, on the anniversary of their meeting, he had given her the first bunch of lilacs and the first proposal.

Ruby opened the card of the nearest lilacs. It read: "Marry me?" The next one over had a card that read: "Marry me not?" It went that way around the room: "Marry me? Marry me not? Marry me?" She stopped opening them after a while, and only removed the cards and tossed them into the trash.

Her eyes were watering. The smell was too much for this small space. Maybe too much for her too. Eden pecked on the door even as Ruby slid onto the chaise by the window.

"Knock knock, yourself," Ruby called, mustering playfulness from somewhere.

Eden came into the room, swaying in Ruby's high heels. "Ta-da," she said, indicating the flowers. "That Paul." Everybody thought Paul Carrigan was better than chocolate.

"That Paul," Ruby echoed, hoping she sounded somewhere near as appreciative as Eden did.

"Should I get him on the phone for you?"

Ruby knew it was the right thing to do. But she couldn't. "No," she told Eden, adding a sexy purr to her tone, "I'll say my thank-yous tonight."

Eden grinned knowingly.

"What'd I miss?" Ruby asked, diverting them both back to business. She could see that Eden had her legal pad smeared up with arrows and exclamation points and big, bold cross-outs.

Eden collapsed into the swivel chair next to Ruby, crossing her legs ostentatiously and swinging the Maud Frizon pumps in the very way Ruby herself was known to do in her sassier moments. Ruby grinned at Eden's homage while her assistant reported the newly released ratings report (still high as the Muckety-Mucks' hopes), the RSVPs that they had to decide on today (yes to the homeless children's benefit, no to the gallery opening), and the press calls Ruby needed to return or to jettison (to do the *Redbook* cover or not? to answer *Entertainment Weekly*'s inquiries about her Hollywood encounter last week with that scruffy Ethan?).

Someone rapped on the door. Trev's head appeared, though he didn't meet Ruby's eye. He was livid about the way she had commandeered the show this morning. "You ready for tomorrow's briefing?" he asked now.

Ruby queried Eden with a look that asked for rescue. Eden barked like a watchdog: "Not now. Her legal team is here."

As Trev backed out, Ruby moaned. "Bone's here?"

"Waiting patiently," Eden confirmed.

"Okay," Ruby said, resigned once again to haggling over what she was worth. Bone was prone to overvaluing her—and getting his price. Which only made her uncomfortable. She had grown up eating Crisco sandwiches on

Wonder Bread and having her mother's dresses made over to fit her, however poorly. She had grown up wearing flip-flops from Wal-Mart and hand-me-down mascara that you had to revive with water from the faucet. But here was Bone, her unlikely Bronx savior morphed into her brilliant strategist, who had himself grown up hungry. Worse, he had grown up short in that East Tremont neighborhood of giants. And it had taught him to fight muscle with brain. It had taught him to fight, to fight, to fight. God, that fight in him had steeled him through high school and City College and through law school. It had made him rich, had put him into Armani and Rolex and Mercedes. It had helped put Ruby into her Maud Frizons too. Filthy, they both called it; he with a smirk on his face because didn't they deserve it, at last? and she with a cocked eyebrow of scorn because didn't they still know it was a sin, having too much when it was possible to have so little?

Bone came in, his eyes glinting behind his little Spike Lee glasses, his hand running down his tie as if he couldn't stop touching the silk of it. Ruby blew him a silent kiss in greeting as her assistant glanced down over her sheet. "One more thing," Eden said. "This guy Mack Lewis from *The Village Voice* has called three times for you and insists that you call him back. *Not me.*" And then, for emphasis, Eden grinned her evil, Jack-Nicholson-in-*The-Shining* grin.

"He's scared of Cinderella, huh?" Ruby teased her.

"He said to tell you he was referred by Len Bottom."

Ruby's laughter almost choked her. She had spent enough time under the television lights to recover herself smoothly. Still, her shock must have shown a little.

Eden paused. Bone looked at her with his street-savvy eyes that telescoped, didn't miss anything.

"Tummy trouble," Ruby explained, patting herself.

"I'll get you some peppermint tea," her assistant told her. Bone settled into his favorite chair.

"And Eden," Ruby said, faking nonchalance, "leave that *Voice* guy's number on my desk. I'll introduce myself." She batted her lashes.

Eden laughed on cue as she closed the door behind her. Bone shook his head in sympathy for the poor sucker who had stepped in this one, and Ruby managed to wink at him, flirting on autopilot because that was all that was left to her: *Len Bottom?*

"Hey, Ruby," Bone said, a grin brimming out of one side of his mouth.

"Hey, Bone," she said. "I see your fin is all polished up."

His grin spread wide enough to show his sharp eye-teeth, though he was no shark—only short Bone still trying to add another inch or two with merely the label of his Gucci loafers. He touched his tie again, as though for luck, scanned his hand-held Newton, and then launched into his latest list of proposed bonuses—this percentage on that, this escalation based on that. She could tell he was proceeding carefully, waiting for her to come unhinged at the audacity of it. But she couldn't react. It was as though she had gone numb except for the spot at the base of her brain where her father's name throbbed: Len Bottom.

Chapter Four

 $\mathcal{T}$ he limo was snarled up in traffic trying to get on the bridge, and Ruby could see Joad zigzagging impatiently behind the wheel, squirming himself because he couldn't find any wiggle room for the Mercedes. In back, she was just as jammed up by her cell phone. She kept hitting redial, three times now, and only to get the *Voice* guy's voice mail, of course. It was impossible to speak to a human anymore. People were all over the streets of Manhattan talking on their cell phones, mocking passersby with their smug insularity. People faxed from airports. They sat on planes and shuffled stock options or hunkered in a ladies' room toilet stall to gossip cryptically into tiny phones. But whenever you had to call anyone, you got a machine.

All she could do was leave a message. And wait. Until tomorrow now. Her afternoon had been gnawed away by Bone and then Trev's team and then by her personal shopper, who had some new things that were "cut from the bolt" for Ruby herself. And by the time Ruby had the time and the privacy to return the call, of course the guy was not going to be at his desk anymore. The *Voice* was a downtown newspaper. Those people didn't really do much work, did they? They were too busy snorting something or shooting something or buying one more black something on St. Mark's Place. They were too busy being snide.

She looked out the window at the gray dusk lowering over the cemeteries that lay on this side of the river. Manhattan itself was already lost in the gloom, lost in the clouds that seemed to have sunk from the weight of the rain until they rested on the city's shoulders. It was a bleak night, made bleaker by her shoes, which were still too tight, and by the lone bouquet of copper-colored lilacs, which she held in her lap. The rest of the flowers, she'd had Eden get rid of. They gave her a headache. She wished for some soothing music, maybe a little Ella. But Joad was up there talking back to that conservative former congressman that NPR always had on. Joad loved listening to "All Things Considered." He hooted at Daniel Pinkwater's dog stories and shook his head in appreciation every time Linda Wertheimer asked a really tough one, and more than once Ruby had seen him puddle up over a story. She would never make him turn off NPR, especially now when he was trapped on the bridge ramp behind a Van Gogh moving truck and the rain was timpani-drumming the windshield. Plus, it had never been her way to put up the window and use her private sound system. It seemed rude, for one thing, and even more isolating, for another. And sad.

Growing up, there had been ten of them in the little house at Shoulderblade. And each brother was worth about two more: loud and full of sap. Led by Raphy, the eldest, they covered that house like a vining weed. If Mama asked them please for once not to pull the apples from her tree, they'd shinny up its trunk, flap all over it like crows, eating the fruit as it hung from the branches, leaving only cores dangling there. Daddy would laugh; they hadn't picked a single apple but they'd eaten their fill. And if he laughed, Mama would too. Wasn't that their downfall, all of them, that she'd just end up laughing too?

Ruby had taught herself to stay awake at night after everyone else was asleep just so she could hear her own sounds. It was on those still midnights that she had promised herself she would someday have a room of her own, a door she could shut tight on a life that belonged only to her, and that then she would sit for hours with nobody's hands in her hair and listen to nothing at all.

But even early on, when she'd found herself at the Bronx apartment on a day when Liza had to be out working, Ruby had wanted the noise of other people. She'd wanted anything to drown out the sound of loneliness, the sound of all she had lost. On Sunday afternoons, she'd sit on her fire escape, just listening to the people downstairs at the neighbor's. She'd sit there until the sun went down and everyone went home and then she'd sit there longer and listen to the sirens and gunfire bursts of laughter from the street and the basketballs backfiring on the asphalt playground. She would listen to the tempo other people's lives made, and know that no matter what she had thought as a little girl with too many brothers and a father who gave too little and a mother who needed too much, the music she made inside herself was never going to be enough.

*O*t was raining harder as Joad broke free of the bridge traffic and headed west into Manhattan. It was a good night to be home with a fire, but something in her longed to keep riding through the nighttime city, looping round and round in the geography of lights. There was an odd, empty comfort in watching the limo's reflection ripple through the streets like some sleek fish in an aquarium made of every storefront window they passed.

"Drive around for a while, could you?" she asked Joad.

He groaned.

"Would you rather come work in the office?" she challenged him with a raised eyebrow aimed right at his mirror.

"Where to?" he asked, slumping his shoulders in mock defeat.

"Circle the park," she decided.

Her fingers touched the little furled blooms, tight as a newborn's fist, and she thought of the lilacs back home, Dewey's lilacs. He had rented that little hillside Victorian in town solely because of the lilac bushes. One of the early settlers in those parts, a Hungarian peddler, had built the white clapboard cottage with its big windows, and his wife, surrounded as she was by all the Scottish and Irish and English immigrants, had been homesick. Her husband must have lugged the lilac bushes, their roots bound in burlap, from all over the north, and she had obviously tended them with great care to make them thrive in the often humid southern air. Her backyard arrangement of the bushes was a triumph, the crescendo of bloom moving with the advancing season along one sloping fence line, up, and then into the high back corner, turning that corner and then going on around until it stopped near the backyard herb garden. Altogether, the blooming lasted a month and a half, while other people's lilac season came and went in a couple of weeks.

The cottage was more than Dewey could afford, really, though it was ramshackle. He was still chipping away at his college loans, would be for a long time to come, and his teaching position barely paid anything. Also, it was more space than he needed, the cottage, all those empty rooms up under the eaves where the shreds of old lace curtains hung in the little arched windows. But he had to take care of those lilacs, had to save them from the deterioration that had set in since the old Hungarian widow's daughter's death. He liked the love story they told, and he liked the rhythm of liming them in the fall and giving them a manure mulch in the spring and another in July after he cut back the dried seed pods so all the energy could go to next year's buds. Gardening kept him reminded of the things you shouldn't forget, he said. When she asked him what, he'd smiled that way he had where his eyebrows did more of the work than his lips, and he'd said only that it was important to remember that it was the things you did months before, or even last year, that determined how things would bloom: "It's about how yesterday goes into tomorrow," he told her.

To celebrate their school play, he had invited the whole cast over for a party. He made lemonade and iced tea with mint pulled from the clump by the porch, and he had asked some of the girls to bring cookies. Ruby was embarrassed not to volunteer, but there were no makings for anything in her mother's kitchen. She came instead with a bunch of flowers picked on her way down the mountain into town. When she gave them to him, he put them in a pickling jar with some bunches of burgundy lilacs. "Look how that yellow vibrates off the purple. See how they shimmy together, dancing-like," he said.

The colors were beautiful together. They did dance. And she thought what a shame it was that she would have missed seeing it altogether if he hadn't shown her how.

That night, Ruby left when everyone else did, said good-bye. But then she came back and sat on his porch in the dark. There was music inside the cottage, some low smoky voice that seemed to sing heartache and hope all at once, heartache and hope wound around each other in a way Ruby knew. In spite of that twining voice, that low music, Dewey heard the creak of the swing and came out the screen door.

"Your face is pale as a moonflower," he said softly as he sat down next to her.

She couldn't say anything. Always before, they had talked together breathlessly. In English class, he had started them off on Hamlet. He had stood up there and read aloud in a voice that resonated in Ruby when she lay in bed at night. Later, walking with him in the evenings between when classes ended and play rehearsals began, she had pressed him to talk about Shakespeare and he had told her why he thought Ophelia was the most tragic girl in all of literature but also why cows were put in the fields around the missile sites ("like canaries in the mines") and why even though it sounded hard on your ears, some heavy metal music came straight from Coleridge's poetry.

Until the week before, Ruby had worshiped Dewey as her mama worshiped Luke on *General Hospital*—from an unfathomable distance. And then they had gone walking up Rain Crow Mountain, and his foot had touched hers while they sat by the mountain brook. After that, he began to seem possible. All the days in between, she had heard his voice inside her even when he was not speaking. She had thought of the bruised sheen of the dark hair that rose from his forehead. She had memorized the way his hand looked when he wrote the words *star-crossed* on the chalkboard. And she had not been able to do anything but come back to his porch after everybody else had gone. Though, sitting there close enough to feel the heat of him in the springtime night, she could not speak. She could only listen to that music from inside the house, to that burred voice that exhaled heartache and hope.

Dewey took her hand finally, gathered it up one finger at a time; it was that slow. She heard the air go out of him in a long, low whistle. "I feel like I've been holding my breath, waiting for this," he told her.

"Tell me a poem," she said, because she didn't want to let anything go ahead and happen, because she was afraid then it would all be over. She didn't even know what she wanted from him, nor how to tell him that she wanted anything beyond hearing him recite something he kept inside him. "Something pretty," she added.

He had seemed to muster his voice from some deep place, and then he had begun: " 'From you have I been absent in the spring . . . ' " The words unfolded in the darkness and seemed to give her light to see him. They were Shakespeare's, he told her later, but she hadn't known that then and hadn't needed to know. All she had needed to know was that those words were coming from that deep place she knew already was in him, that place in him where she wanted most to be, to stay. She listened as he finished: " 'Yet seemed it winter still, and, you away, As with your shadow I with these did play.' "

She didn't say anything.

"Was it pretty enough?" he asked.

"Yes," she said. "Tell me another."

"Your turn," he whispered. "You tell me one."

"I don't know anything."

"Sure you do."

"I don't."

"Try."

The swing went back and forth, his one leg moving them in a pendulum that marked the ticking seconds of the night. The only thing she could think to recite was an old schoolyard game that had grown like a chain from one generation to the next as one barefoot child reached for another and sang as she herself had sung, going round and round in the dust of a dozen Augusts.

"Go on," he coaxed her.

She took a breath and recited:

> *"The needle's eye that does supply,*
> *The thread that runs so true,*
> *Many a beau, have I let go,*
> *Because I wanted you."*

She waited for Dewey to laugh at the childish ditty, to laugh at her for not knowing anything better, for not knowing Shakespeare or Donne or even anything in the Bible but John 3:16. He didn't laugh.

"Keep going," he asked gravely.

> *"Many a dark and stormy night,*
> *When I went home with you,*
> *I stumped my toe and down I go,*
> *Because I wanted you."*

"Because I wanted you," he echoed.

She leaned over and kissed him then, and it lasted a long time. It lasted until the swing had swung down and stopped moving at all, like a clock that had lost its tension. Time had stopped.

Dawn was an ember in the eastern sky when Ruby got up from the swing and walked back up the mountain to Shoulderblade and slipped into bed just before her brothers started stretching their muscles to meet the day. Dewey was something in her blood after that, and from then on, he was always going to be humming through her. He was always going to be the cold of a springtime brook and the warmth of another body. He was always going to be the scent of lilacs. He was always going to be the sound of music after dark.

CHAPTER FIVE

*P*aul Carrigan had his lanky frame stretched out flat on Ruby's best Marrakesh kilim. He was wearing his red-heeled wool socks and frayed jean cutoffs, an outfit he perpetually wore in the apartment no matter what season it was outside. He was watching a *Star Trek* rerun and reading a biography of Churchill during commercials. When he heard Ruby come in and close the door, he rolled over and beamed at her. She grinned back, melodramatically wrenching off her pumps.

"Did you ever go to the movies with Senator Spencer?" he asked.

"No," she said, wondering if he had decided to develop a jealous streak after all these years.

"Damn," he said, rolling back over onto his stomach. "We came up with this theory today that everyone sits in a theater according to his politics."

She rolled her eyes playfully, relieved. His biochemical research team was funded by the government (and supplemented by his own father) to do high-tech studies toward finding a cancer cure. But he and his colleagues were always buoying their spirits with nonsensical social experiments.

Paul continued: "You know how I always like to go right to the middle, and that's how I am: centrist. But Horowitz is a complete liberal, and he says that he goes all the way to the left side, all the way. So we came up with this whole scenario, where Newt and his cronies hug the right wall, and the Kennedy clan is passing popcorn up and down the left, and Clinton is bouncing all over the theater, can't get comfortable here, the view seems better from there . . ."

"Oh, Paul . . ." she scoffed lightly, humoring him.

"But you blew it," he teased, "because you were going to prove our theory. You and Spencer."

"Sorry."

"Nice flowers," he said, nodding toward the lilacs.

"Aren't they?" she said, pursing her lips and blowing a kiss his way.

He grabbed her ankle as she walked past, headed toward the bedroom. He tried to bite her on the calf, but she broke away and shed her clothes piece by piece as she made for her dressing room.

"Is this an in or an out celebration?" he called after her, knowing better than to try to get too close before she had stripped off everything that clung to her of the studio, represented by the control-top panty hose and the hip-hugging skirt and the bra with the lace that grew teeth as the day wore on.

"Definitely an in," she answered.

"Which ethnicity?"

"Definitely Chinese, don't you think?" she said as she pulled a cashmere sweatshirt over her head.

"Szechuan, I think."

"Definitely Szechuan," she echoed.

She sat in front of her mirror longer than she should have. Dread hung over her like the sword of Damocles, dangling by a thread. She did not look any different from the woman who had risen this morning and shouldered against the dream back into her world. She did not look any different from the woman who had defied Trev and done her show her way. She looked like the woman who could face all of it, who *had* faced it all and faced it down, and who could do the same with whatever happened tonight, whatever was going to happen tomorrow. But she did not feel like that woman. She felt instead like the desperate teenager she had been, a girl mad with grief and hobbled by Wal-Mart flip-flops.

Paul announced the arrival of the food in what she guessed was either Mandarin or Szechuan. He didn't know that much of either language, but she often teased him that he got a lot of mileage out of what he did know. By the time she got in there, he had the cartons of food lined up on the high gloss of the Edwardian dining room table. She checked to make sure he had placemats under everything.

Of course he did, and he tweaked her for even doubting him. He knew how protective she was of the table's finish. It was carved Asian mahogany, from trees long extinct, and it had been the hinge of many a joke in his family since Ruby had bid on it at Sotheby's. It wasn't that it didn't fit the apartment. It did, tying together the high, ornate ceiling with the polished floors and their marquetry borders. It was only that it didn't fit Ruby and Paul, really.

Neither of them cooked. They didn't boil water. They didn't put popcorn in the microwave. They didn't even have a microwave. And their refrigerator was empty except for several dozen bottles of vitamins. They did own crystal and china because Ruby saw the decorative appeal of having it displayed behind beveled glass in the magnificent break-front (from an auction in Saugerties), and they owned silver because his father said it was a good investment. But their vast European-style kitchen was equipped with little more than a corkscrew. Whatever they craved, they ordered in. Or they went out.

Paul whistled around the table, assembling one mu shu pancake for himself and one for her. They loaded up their Limoges plates with cold sesame noodles and egg rolls and General Tso's chicken. They popped open cold beer. Then they sat down on the floor cross-legged in front of the television. Paul scooped with his chopsticks, slurping. Ruby twirled noodles around a silver fork from eighteenth-century England. They didn't talk. They never did.

Ruby ate the cold noodles first, the long strands studded with preserved garlic so pungent it was sweet. She ate the egg rolls, two of them. She cut each piece of chicken into little bits so that she could savor it longer. When Paul went back for more, she did too. She ate as though she were eating salvation.

She hadn't eaten much all day, never did. There was the occasional rice cake at the office, and she would pick at a salad or a piece of fish when Eden ordered in for a lunch meeting. Not eating wasn't about fat grams or cellulite. It wasn't about anorexia or size-six dresses. It was about keeping herself sharp, her mind hewed to a fine edge by the rub of hunger. It was how she had done her homework, how she'd taken the college-entrance exams. And she secretly believed that it was what had gotten her where she was. But at night, it was different. With Paul, it was different. She could relax, disappear into her food. Eating was not just about nourishment for her, and Paul understood that somehow. He had from the beginning. It had been Chinese carry-out then too.

Looking back, Ruby thought Paul had watched her eating that first night and learned everything he needed to know about her. There had been one moment: Her mu shu pancake had leaked plum sauce down her hand, and she had licked it off unself-consciously, as she would've in complete solitude. Only it had struck her in that instant that she wasn't alone, and she had looked up to make sure he hadn't noticed. Only he had. He was grinning at her. And then he held his own pancake over his head and caught a mushroom as it oozed out.

That was the moment that sealed it, though they had met earlier in the night, after her first college party. She had not expected the party to be like a barn ruckus back home, where by night's end the homemade liquor obliterated everything but itself. And it wasn't like that. But it was so much quieter than anything she would've imagined, merely a drone of conversation that rose and fell along with the classical music on the stereo. It made her feel loud all over. She seemed to clang in that Central Park West apartment: the flowered blouse she had borrowed from Liza, her red hair billowing out in the humid air, her spurts of laughter that were as bold as she was insecure. Finally, she edged her way to an open window and stayed near it, holding her first glass of wine ever, holding it for security, really, because the golden liquid tasted sour as medicine to her. It grew warm in her hand. She stayed there where she could see the trees in the park tossing their swollen leaf buds in gusts of strong wind, and it calmed her as she talked to the men who sparked conversations. Each spoke at first about the university or the city, and each ended by some variation of asking—and it was their drinks talking, she knew—if she wanted to go someplace quiet.

Other women didn't offer anything but sidelong glances, and Ruby began to feel very aware of the low cut of her blouse. In lieu of parting the thick crowd to escape, she began to project all her hope onto a single man. He snagged her glance every time her eyes skittered away from the latest proposition and out across the room like a rabbit flushed out of hiding. His own eyes seemed kind each time they caught hers that way, and after he approached, he seemed nice and interested that she was from Kentucky and curious to know how she happened to find her way to the city. He drew her out small-talking about Columbia and himself. But as the conversation wore on, she began to feel uncomfortable. He asked her questions rapid-fire without letting her catch her breath between them, without letting her carefully consider her answers. She did not recover, one to the next. They were all over her like groping hands, his questions. She was feeling oddly exposed. And that was what later she couldn't forgive herself, that she had ignored her own good sense and instead had naively allowed herself to be forced out into the open, where he had been able to pick her off with one shot.

She was smiling when it happened. A colleague of his had approached them. "You'll never believe," her acquaintance said. "We've got our very own ambassador from Appalachia here, come north to get educated. Would you believe her name? It's the very model of mountain nomenclature. It's Ruby Blossom Bottom. Tell us again how they arrived at it," he said, "your ma and pa."

Her name grew pitted in the acid of his cruelty, dissolving along with her self-esteem. He turned a smile on her, though, one eyebrow raised. And they all laughed together. Ruby too. She laughed longer and louder than either of the others, though she could already feel something thudding around inside her, threatening to break her apart from the inside out.

"You'll have to excuse me," she said, as the men coursed blithely on to a discussion of the failed economics of Appalachian coal mining. She wanted to say something loud and bawdy, something hillbilly about needing to be shown the way to the outhouse, please. She wanted them to know she got the joke but didn't find it funny. But it was all she could do to smile a polite good-bye and push her way to the door and down in the elevator and out.

There were tears in her eyes by the time she got to the street, the first she'd allowed herself since she had come north. Not that she really allowed these. They just came, and the harsh, barely April wind whipped them back across her temples. She felt disoriented, couldn't tell uptown from down, couldn't remember where the subway stop was. All that seemed clear and solid was a bench across the street, under the overhanging trees in the park. And so she crossed with the light and stumbled toward some peace, a respite. The whole park gave off the green light of the gas lamps as they cast dark shadows from the trees. Two shapes emerged from the nightshade, reaching toward her. She recoiled and knew with a blast of cold conviction that she had stumbled from one danger into something worse. But she was so tired, so ground down by unrelenting regret. She had not stopped moving since the day she stepped on the bus in Jackson. She had not stopped running away from too many things and toward too many others. She couldn't keep it straight anymore, who she was and who she wanted to be, couldn't keep it clear in her mind because she was so often confronted by the inescapability of who everyone else would think she was based solely on who she had been. Her own name had betrayed things about her behind her back. She hadn't even known what it was saying about her. So, now as the men (for they were men and they were so close she could see their fierce faces) reached for her, she didn't resist. Maybe it was all she deserved.

A sudden voice rose up above the wind, deep and pitched hard. If she heard the words she could never remember what they were. She did remember first the hands and next the men themselves dissolving back into shapes and then back into the darkness. She remembered turning and seeing the tall silhouette of a man under the streetlight, a man rushing toward her. He reached for her, held her protectively. She could feel her heart hammering against him and felt that she should be frightened but wasn't. "You okay?" he whispered into her hair.

She nodded.

"I saw you leave the party."

She looked up at him then, afraid suddenly that he was one of the men who had come on to her and that she was doing it again, being naive, too trusting. But his face was one she didn't recognize, full of the dark hollows that nighttime provides a face made of angles and planes and deep-set eyes. Even so, it was gentle. She knew that, knew it from the tough part of herself that had climbed onto that bus and found the Bronx apartment and claimed admission to Barnard. She knew it from the part of herself that was most sure of itself: This man was gentle.

They walked across the park, and she wasn't fearful. He seemed to be all that was required as barrier between herself and whatever, whomever, had skulked out of sight. Together, they crossed a hollow of darkness, draped round by a constellation of windows in a city that seemed more sky than steel beams and poured concrete and blueprint geometry. The trees were seething with the wind. And the clouds moving among the towers of the skyscrapers were orange and blue and gold from the reflected light. The two of them didn't say anything as they walked, but he took her hand when she tripped over a stone in the cobbled path, and he kept it as they moved back into the obscurity under the trees on the East Side and then out onto Fifth Avenue.

Paul, his name was Paul Carrigan, and he had taken her up to the penthouse he had inherited from his grandparents and opened the door on a space that echoed. He had a mattress on the floor and toppling stacks of *National Geographic*s. Heavy science textbooks were studded like columns around the room, arranged by area of study, he told her. There was not a single piece of furniture, not one.

She had wandered from room to room in a kind of ecstatic disbelief. Ruby had been awed by the architecture at the university, thought it majestic. When she had first seen the Cathedral of St. John the Divine she had been like a French peasant coming across the countryside and looking up to see Chartres, so imposing that only God himself could have placed it there. But the cathedral with its bristling spires and the law library at Columbia with its cascade of stairs, these were public buildings. She had never guessed that grandeur was something that could house the everyday rituals. She found it unbelievable that Paul Carrigan opened his eyes, yawned, and stretched each morning under this ceiling dripping with wedding-cake plaster. He merely shrugged off her amazement. His parents' place was no different from this.

It was after she circled three times through the apartment like an orbiting planet, it was after she had knelt to touch the pattern of the wood floors and run her hands along the built-in bookcases that Paul punched Bryan Ferry's recording into the stereo. Then, she stopped, listened to the music that echoed what she had felt about Manhattan as she walked across Central Park at midnight. She had stood at the window, staring out into the misty night where the car lights blurred into a river of red and white. It's like living in a treehouse, she thought. Everything's down there, shrunken to nothing that matters at all. And in that moment, she had started to hope that someday, some way she could make right what had gone so wrong.

He hadn't asked any questions. He was the kind of guy who could talk for fifteen minutes on the kinds of red peppers used in Szechuan cooking—and did when their carry-out food was delivered. He talked about the peppers ("not for eating") and then about the street food in China and then about this little kid he had seen in Tiananmen Square wearing nothing but a diaper and a pair of those little bird-faced slippers made of silk.

That was about the time she licked the plum sauce off her hand. And after they finished eating, they got up off the floor and danced close together in the almost-dark. There was only the light from the streetlights below. There was only the whisper of their stocking feet moving on the hardwood floors. There was only his strong body moving against hers, the two of them tall and perfectly matched. And there was this new music in the night that seemed to haunt her with old promises.

*N*ow here they were years later, stretched out from opposite ends of a sectional couch, cozy in that cavernous apartment she had made into a home. He was rubbing her feet, watching the third sitcom in a row on *Nick at Night*. She looked at him, the colors of the television playing over his face as he laughed at the onscreen silliness. He had a mild countenance, matching his day-to-day temperament. His hair was blond as a child's and fine that way too. His one strong feature was a right-angle jaw, determined. It wasn't misleading. Most of life he moved through with the ease of the wealth he had been born into. He read the biographies he loved and never missed *Star Trek* in syndication. He prided himself on knowing by heart the phone number of twenty different takeout places. He would've been just as comfortable right now watching Mary Tyler Moore from that old mattress on the floor of an empty apartment instead of from this expensive couch. He had not been born into a world where it was left for him to prove anything. But as the set of his jaw implied, he would not be refused certain things. His was the kind of tenacity possessed by children of privilege—every effort paid off in the end: You want the go-cart at F. A. O. Schwarz, only ask. You want to go around the world after college, and so be it. Now, Paul Carrigan wanted to find a cure for cancer. Also he wanted Ruby.

Out of all the men at that long-ago party, she had not even noticed him. She knew it for sure later that night when she saw his face in the light. But his presence had stood from that time forward between her and everything else that might have been. In the early months of their relationship, she had come and gone from his apartment, from his life, like cloud shadows passing across the park. She had not told him her real name but the name she wanted to be real. She had not told him that she was going home from his Upper East Side penthouse to the recklessly dangerous streets of the South Bronx. She would never have told him that. After what had happened to her at that party, she had quickly learned to take haven in omission.

But then Liza had disappeared. Ruby had caught her cousin crying several times in the last month, and Liza sometimes went out of the apartment without curling her hair, without putting on stockings. She complained about her clothes smelling like kielbasa after work, about the city air always stinking like burned coffee. "Crud!" she'd curse when any little thing went wrong. "Crud, crud, crud!" in a crescendo of disproportionate anger.

Ruby sat in the apartment that night. She sliced tomatoes from the elderly neighbor lady's fire-escape garden and salted them, but Liza never came home to eat supper or to sleep. All her things were there, her treasures: the blouse so smooth you could almost pretend it was real silk, the sling-back pumps one size too big that somebody had left in the restaurant where she worked, the pictures of the boy she had loved back home. Ruby had paced the apartment from one end to another, looking out into the orange glow of the city and wondering where under that unnatural sky, where was her cousin? The neighbor lady called after her the next morning when she hurtled down the stairs, "What was wrong that you was pawin' like a cat overhead all the night long?" The poor woman still had her hair wrapped in a bright bandana, and she looked like someone who hadn't slept and who was going to know why. But when Ruby told her about Liza, her irritation disappeared. "Oh, honey," she said, with both hands at her throat. "You go to the police. You go now."

But the police had other things to worry about, and Bone was out-of-bounds in Manhattan, taking midterms. So in desperation Ruby went to the East Side. Outside

Paul's building, she hesitated. She circled the block once, trying to decide. But she knew already that he was her only hope. So she had gone up in the elevator. His features had lifted and brightened to see her unexpectedly and then clouded over as he read the fear written all over her.

He had a scientist's mind. It rose above the churning of hers and approached the problem empirically. He made her sit down, made her breathe in and out, made her tell him what facts she knew. Then he had taken her by the hand. They had driven downtown.

Liza had waited tables the day before, her boss said, done her whole shift, taken her paycheck, and left. Same smile on the way out the door, same wiggle of her fingers waving. "She's a good girl, that Liza," he told them. "Dresses like the worst sort, but you can't judge that way."

Ruby was already thinking that of course the worst sorts of men did judge that way, whether you deserved it or not. She began to sob into her hands, and Paul insisted that they go to her apartment so he could take a look at things. "Where am I going?" he said, heading uptown along Third Avenue.

That had only made her cry harder. She had worked so hard at her own illusion. Now it was going with Liza. She couldn't get the words out. But he held north anyway. He took the Willis Avenue Bridge, made an exit into the South Bronx, found her street. When she asked how he had known where she lived, he shrugged, looked sheepish. "I followed you once," he said. He wouldn't elaborate. That's when she knew how much he cared for her, how much she meant to him and not just the other way around. She reached over and squeezed his leg, feeling the thigh muscle tighten as he resolutely accelerated.

They clattered together up the stairs, past the poor neighbor, whose sober countenance foretold that they weren't going to find Liza home. And they didn't. It was as though she had simply evaporated. Ruby walked around Liza's half of the bedroom. She touched the comb Liza had used for a hundred strokes every night, the framed pictures, the scarfs hanging makeshift around the window like some exotic curtains. She shuffled through the stack of pictures, which Liza had saved every dime to have taken and which hadn't yet got her a job modeling.

When the sun began to set, Paul made her leave a note for Liza and come home with him. They sat in the twilight of his unlit apartment, and he asked her questions and met the answers without judgment. She told him what she could about how she had grown up, let him guess what he would. She didn't tell him the worst of it, knew she never could. He wouldn't be able to look at her after that. He would feel about her then the way she felt about herself. He would let go of her, set her adrift again in the awful recognition of what she had tried to leave behind in Kentucky. He would let go of her, and she would lose her only hope. Her new life would fail as miserably as her old.

After listening until she had wound down to a profound silence, he had waited a while, only stroking her hair. And then he suggested that maybe Liza had gone back to Kentucky.

"Why on earth?" Ruby asked as though it were the most preposterous idea possible. There was a tone in her voice that accused him of not really listening if he could even suggest it. "Why would she want to go and do something like that?"

"Because it's home," Paul said.

Ruby realized then that he had heard more than her words describing the poverty and the hardship; he had heard what murmured deepest in her, heard her longing for home. If even she could harbor such a love for the mountains, what must Liza have kept hidden away in her heart? Ruby had gone about saving herself, climbing into fresh circumstances here. But Liza was living the same hardscrabble struggle as back home, only without the familiar faces and voices and ways. Liza was just lost in a strange city, and every day she had felt more the loss of her cousin. As Ruby had grown large in her new life, Liza had shrunk to nothing.

The next day Ruby had dialed her aunt's house in Kentucky. The phone had rung once, twice, again. And then Liza had answered. Ruby didn't say anything to her cousin. She just pressed her finger on the button, hung up. Liza was safe. She had gone without saying anything. Ruby would leave it that way.

They went back to the Bronx to pack up. All of Liza's belongings got folded into a Gallo wine box that Ruby addressed and sent to Zachariah County. Ruby's things, including her textbooks, fit into only the two duffels that Paul had brought with him.

The neighbor lady kissed her on the cheek and sent her away with a beefsteak tomato that filled Ruby's entire hand. She and Paul ate it sliced with salt that night. And she had never lived anywhere but with him since.

$\mathcal{P}$aul aimed the remote at the television and clicked it off. Silence fell over them. He looked at her, then pointed the remote toward the stereo, clicked again. Bryan Ferry's voice filtered around them, tuned low.

"Happy anniversary, Ruby," he said with a duskiness in his voice that betrayed the deepened emotion he felt.

"Happy anniversary," she answered. She was holding his gaze, but she wanted to look away, wanted to swerve away from what was coming. But she was so tired. The dream this morning, the lilacs, the phone call today had just pushed her too far, shoved her hard and way beyond her endurance. After all these years, she was just too tired.

Paul took her hand and led her to the middle of the floor, where he gathered her against him. She felt the power of him, the strength that came not from weight lifting or running in the park but from the absolute surety of who he was and what he was capable of in this world, that came from the certainty of knowing what he wanted.

What he wanted was in his arms, had been for the past

seven years. But she wouldn't give herself to him, wouldn't say she'd never leave. She wouldn't marry him.

"You haven't said much about the flowers," he whispered.

"They're beautiful," she said. They turned in circles on the carpet. Her face was in the hollow of his neck. She felt his pulse there, steady and sure.

"Will you?" he asked.

They pivoted together, his arms holding her up, still holding her up.

"Will you, Ruby?"

"Yes," she exhaled, feeling something in her rise like the last smoke from an extinguished candle. "Yes."

CHAPTER SIX

*R*uby opened the papers on her desk the next morning to discover that she had been Page Sixed. Someone had betrayed her to the *Post*'s gossip columnists. Eden materialized and stood over Ruby as she read the item, which salivated over a tip from insiders that Ruby's ego had inflated until it was commensurate with her network broadcast coverage. She squandered money on bringing in ten guests and by caprice whittled them down to two, it tittered. She wouldn't heed the expertise of her highly paid staff. She was erratic. She was petulant. "The sugar-coated hostess has become a bitter pill to swallow," it concluded smugly.

"Ouch," Ruby breathed.

"Did he really think you wouldn't know who had leaked that?" Eden asked.

"Probably doesn't care."

And the funny thing was, Ruby didn't know how

much she herself cared. Not after last night. She *was* capricious. She *was* erratic. She had intended to tell Paul no. But saying yes had been so simple. Putting off the saying no until tomorrow had been so, so simple. Her fortune cookie had warned her, "Procrastinating puts your fate on hold." But she had only gone on procrastinating. This morning as she stood over Paul, she knew she should wake him and tell him that she wasn't going to marry him, that for better or worse, she couldn't. She had looked at his fair lashes in the morning light, at the divet of tender skin at his temple, had even reached her hand to his shoulder. But in the end, she had only stooped and kissed him, made her lipstick mark on him, left. As usual.

And now, with her fate still on hold, she folded up the *Post* and tossed it in the trash, slipping into her routine just as she slipped into the Tahari dress that wardrobe had chosen for her. She got into her groove. She quipped with Fritz and admired his new frames (number 207), drank her Evian, quibbled over which accessories to wear. And then she took the stage, brushed off Trev's last-minute admonitions, and greeted her audience. She segued gracefully from one verbal stunt to the next. All as usual.

But she felt exposed. Standing there, she felt something riven through the shell that she had built brick by brick around her. As long as everyone seemed to believe in her, it was easier to believe in herself. It was easier to believe that she was what the papers said she was, what for all the world she appeared to be. Now as she tried to hold it together, she was too aware that others could squint into the dark crevice and see her, huddled in the carapace of her success, so very small.

ℳ

*W*hen she got back to the office, Eden had tallied up Ruby's morning calls: her publicist, her trainer, Bone (twice). There were dozens of press calls regarding the *Post* item (none Ruby could face returning). Not one of the calls came from downtown at the *Voice*.

The phone on her desk clicked again. Eden plucked it up, turned it over to Ruby, who leapfrogged from one phone call to the next for two hours: She tried to concentrate on placating the Muckety-Mucks, who were taking her temperature, gauging if Page Six was simple office politics or a more dire power play. She laughed off the item, played it down, swatted it into insignificance. The whole time, she was watching the lights flash on her phone and bracing herself for Mack Lewis. But he was aggressively not calling.

Finally, she couldn't stand it anymore. She felt sure she would deal better with everything if she could just get an explanation for this Len Bottom thing. It had to be a mistake; just let her get it cleared up and she'd be fine. She punched line two. If he wouldn't return her call, she'd preempt him. Ignoring the other line's ringing, Ruby began dialing.

Eden buzzed. "Gracie's on line two," she said.

Ruby's index finger hovered over the last digit of Mack Lewis's phone number: Paul's mother.

In the cottony release of her assent last night, she hadn't thought to tell Paul to keep it to himself. She had thought she would just reverse herself in the morning and that would be that. But she hadn't told him no this morning. And now she was sure he had gone and told his mother yes. Her fate was on hold, blinking persistently on line one.

"I'll take it," she sighed.

She punched the line-one button. "Gracie?" she said buoyantly. Amazing what a few acting lessons could do for you.

"Darling, we could not be more thrilled," Paul's mother gushed. "If we had to go out and buy a daughter from all the ones on the rack at Bergdorf's, my dear, you would be the one and only."

Ruby laughed. Paul's mother was her son's opposite, given to hyperbole and high energy. Though Ruby had been raised with a strong prejudice against high rollers (as her daddy invariably called rich people), she had found that Paul's family had an intellectual curiosity that kept their minds propped open just a little farther than others in their tax bracket. The father, Paul Two, had once gone to elaborate lengths to capture a luna moth that fluttered at a window of their country house, a moth so big it wouldn't die easily. The next day, he had actually taken it to a vet to have it chloroformed—all because his young Paul had an insect collection. Now, Paul Two bankrolled much of his son's cancer research, and Gracie herself fund-raised for the Egyptian wing at the Met because she had as a girl studied anthropology. Paul bragged to everyone that she had once gone on a dig along the Nile. "That mother of mine has King Tut dust under her fingernails," he'd say to his buddies whenever Gracie was around to benefit from the boasting.

But no such dust could possibly continue to cling under Gracie Carrigan's nails. She went to her manicurist three times a week, each time ending with a pastel pink polish called Seashell. Her hair was helped-along blond, and her face had been tucked into shape more than once. She was tall and elegant and refined, so refined, in fact, that she had never pressed for details about Ruby's past. For that one favor, Ruby forgave her the rhinoplasty and the pedicures and the retro lettuce lunches at Mortimer's.

"Now, here's the plan . . ."

Of course there would already be a plan.

"Grandma Rose is coming up from Palm Beach on Friday," Gracie was saying. "She is positively thrilled. If you haven't heard from her, you will. She sees it as a fine excuse to finally witness what you've done with the apartment."

"But—"

"Now, don't protest, darling. I know you want to keep things simple. Paul has given me instructions already. But what if we were to do just a nice family gathering, an engagement party at your place on Saturday? Now, don't panic. It's high time, and I'll take care of every detail, you know I will. We'll have the Conrads and the Plummers and the Meyers, just a few close family friends, you understand. And family, of course. I know Meredith will insist on coming from L.A., and I don't suppose we can help it if the Shelleys want to pop down from Boston. . . ."

Ruby was getting disabled by dizziness. Gracie rocketed on with her plans and her expectations and her goodwill, and Ruby thought, *They own me.* Only, how could she suddenly belong to Paul, belong to the Carrigans from Palm Beach to Beverly Hills to Park Avenue? How could she belong to anyone but . . . ?

"Now I want you to get everything written down for me and fax it over," Gracie was saying, "and I'll take care of notifying the *Times.* You'll tell your publicist that this is something for a mother to take care of. We want the *Times* to have it first, of course, dear, and then your publicity people can do their thing."

"Hold up a minute, Gracie," Ruby got in finally. "Listen, I don't want to disappoint you, but we can't go rushing ahead like this. There are some things I have to take care of."

"What things?" There was a red tinge of alarm around the rosiness of her tone.

Ruby groped. "I'm in the middle of contract negotiations, Gracie. You can understand that I need to soft-pedal my private life right now, not give them any major life changes to worry about. They've got me hooked up to emotional seismography equipment, you know, my own little Richter scale."

"This doesn't have anything to do with that young actor, Ethan what's-his-name?" Gracie asked.

"Gracie!" Ruby rebuked her playfully. "You know that's nothing but my PR firm's antics."

"Won't they tone it down if you're married? I mean . . . for Paul's sake, at least, won't you ask them?"

"Of course, but I need to handle this my way. Just now."

"Of course." Gracie's tone was tight as her lips after a face-lift. Ruby thought she was off the hook, but then Paul's mother added, ever relentless: "But the party, dear? Surely we can forge ahead with that, perhaps just prune it back to no one but the immediate family?"

Once again, Ruby hesitated, then assented—for no reason but the momentary relief it would provide. And when she hung up the receiver, she sat with her head in her hands, feeling her weakness, the weakness that had caused so much damage, too much. The phone must've clicked, the intercom must've buzzed, but she didn't hear anything. The next thing she knew, Eden was at her side.

"Need an Advil?" her assistant asked.

Ruby nodded.

Eden said, "That guy from the *Voice* is on hold, but I'll get rid of him. I can see you're in no mood."

Ruby's head snapped up. "No," she said too quickly. "I'll take it. Hold everything else."

CHAPTER SEVEN

*T*oad slapped the wheel and snorted in amusement when she told him where she wanted to go. "You do know that is below Fifty-seventh Street?" he asked with a wry smirk.

She smiled gamely.

"And it's not Soho," he added pointedly.

"No?" She played along.

"There are people of color down there," he said in a confidential whisper. He loved to needle her about living in the homogenous enclave of upper Fifth Avenue while he went home every night to the more colorful and therefore more wonderful West Side.

She rolled her eyes. "Hush up and drive."

He chuckled as he steered toward the bridge and Manhattan. "You are a whole bunch of surprises, aren't you?" he asked.

"A whole bunch," she echoed, staring out the window. But she didn't take up a conversation.

Ruby had never been to Alphabet City in her life. But how bad could it be? It was, after all, technically part of the Village. Okay, so it was the part where the homeless rioted against police for sleeping rights in some park. She gathered it was not the Greenwich Village of ivy-wound fences and antique brick buildings with shutters on weak hinges. But Ruby had lived in the South Bronx. And if she had to go to Avenue B to meet Mack Lewis in some bar, then she was willing.

As the blocks clicked by, counting down as if toward some bomb blast, she kept repeating to herself that Mack Lewis's story didn't really add up, couldn't. He couldn't really have anything, not given what he'd said on the phone. But how did he know her father's name?

Looking out the window, she began to be aware of how her sleek black Mercedes contrasted with the tough neighborhood. She anticipated how she herself would stand out with her flaming hair, her close-cut Chanel, her famous face.

"Are you sure you've got the address right?" Joad asked her. She had felt his eyes shift again and again to her in the rearview mirror, checking on her more often than usual. He was sitting up straighter, seemed more alert.

"I'm sure," she said. She was nervous too. But she didn't want him to see it.

The limo was stopped at a red light. People on the corners were looking at it. A man with a trash bag of bottles over his shoulder touched the hood ornament on his way across the street.

"You know what," Ruby said, "we're gonna change our plan here a little, Joady." She was thinking fast, grappling with all her fears, giving one priority over another. She had to meet this guy. But she didn't want to be recognized. Personal safety came last, given her choices. She could take care of herself. If she had done it at age seventeen, she could do it now.

"I'm gonna hop out at the next corner. And then I'm gonna meet you in an hour at the corner of Fifth Avenue and Washington Square, there by the arch."

"You're gonna what?" he began, clearly opposed to putting her out in this neighborhood.

She berated herself. She should've been more chatty, less self-absorbed on the ride over. He could read her the way he could read trouble between the lines in *Variety*, way before it ever hit the headlines. Joad knew something was wrong.

"One hour, Joady," she instructed in a tone that was more authoritarian than any she had ever used with him. "I've got my cell phone if I need you."

With that, she stepped out into the street, pulling her charmeuse scarf over her hair. Her eyes were shuttered behind dark Armani glasses. "Garbo does Alphabet City," she wisecracked to herself as she crossed the street, heading downtown. She saw the limo slink around the next corner. He was taking his time getting out of sight.

She concentrated on placing her heels carefully on the rough sidewalk. *Step on a crack, break your mother's back,* some inner voice chanted. Strange what came back.

Somebody whistled from a second-story window. She kept her head down, kept her pace steady. Her only hope was that she could pass for a neighborhood drag queen who'd outdone himself. It was possible. Ruby knew she had the same kind of overblown rose looks, and she did stand six feet in heels. One of her favorite shows had been the one she did with RuPaul, the two of them an elegant match. As she walked, she concentrated on being a man being a woman. The exercise got her through the last block. "You go, girl," she prodded herself in RuPaul's voice.

The bar glowered on the corner, practically unmarked except for a neon bottle in the window. She hesitated as the smell of old spilled beer washed out of the doorway, like the surf emerging from an oceanside cave. She pulled breath down into her diaphragm and stepped in.

It was gloomy, and she had to lift her glasses to get the lay of the place. A few men at the bar turned away from the television to note her entrance. They stared. Her eyes ricocheted off them, trying to catch it if one of them registered welcome but trying not to welcome any other advances. Finally, she saw a hand waving from a back booth and moved toward it.

"You found the place," the man said to her. He was

younger than she had thought he was going to be. Or looked younger anyway, pudgy in the cheeks.

"You're Mack," she said.

He nodded. When she had finally found his name in the *Voice*, it was as a byline on a cartoon, a cartoon populated by spiky, pen-scrawled characters who had little balloons over their heads filled with sardonic observations on the local human drama. Mack Lewis was the kind of caricaturist who foisted people onto the tip of his pen, skewered them so that they squirmed on the page like pinned insects on velvet. He reduced life into four little squares, no room for nuance or extenuating circumstances, no excuses.

She reached for his hand, grasped it tightly, shook it warmly. "I'm so thrilled to meet you," she said, her voice hushed way off its normal volume. "I admire your work." Her lips twitched involuntarily. This was not the most cool she had ever been in her life.

She smiled at him, and he smiled back, though it was one of those lopsided, arch kind of things that sent an ambiguous message. He might have been smiling with her, or he might have been smiling smugly at her brazen and transparent attempt to flatter him. He was nothing if not downtown. His hair was shorn to a bristle that matched the growth on his chin, and his ear was spiked with a row of pewter studs. His fingernails were chewed back to the quick, and they were rimmed with ink. It was his eyes she fastened her hope on, his brown liquid eyes set deep in the unhealthy puffiness of his pitted face. She thought now that the pudginess wasn't youth, it was alcoholism.

"Do you want a drink?" he asked her.

"A beer?"

"Hey, Jud," he yelled to the guy behind the bar. "Shoot us over another one."

The guy came around and put the sweating bottle in front of Ruby, then stood over her. She smiled up at him, then realized he wanted his money then and there.

Money? She panicked for a minute. She never carried much cash on her, never had a reason to, really. She fumbled in her purse, thankfully found some loose singles, the change from when she sent Eden to get chocolate sorbet at Häagen-Dazs last time she had PMS. As she held the money out to the barkeeper, the irony of the bills passing from her manicured fingers into his rough palm was not lost on her. She hated the juxtaposition, felt it cost her with Mack. And this performance was for him.

He was a tough audience. He studied her as she took a long swig of her Bud. She had faltered there, looking for cash. She wanted her strength back.

"So about your pop . . ." Mack began.

"Isn't that the weirdest thing?" she said. "These people just come out of the woodwork when you're on television. Nobody ever talks about that, really, don't want to insult all the decent fans. But there are a lot of crazies who gnaw away on you. Like termites."

"Yeah, well, he didn't really sound like your typical crazy."

"What do you mean?"

"Well, he was sitting in here one day, at the bar, watching your show on the television. Right over there." He motioned to a corner seat, and she followed the gesture. The bar stool was empty.

"He was sitting over there with his face fixated on that television screen. And the tears were just dripping off his chin," Mack continued. "They were really dropping into his liquor: *plunk, plunk, plunk,* like that. And I couldn't help being interested because I've never really seen anybody crying in their beer, you know, and it's the kind of thing a cartoonist can use. . . ."

Ruby's heart began to thud. Crying?

It was him. It was her dad. He never could get drunk without weeping. Or worse.

Ruby didn't even blink.

Mack went on: "I'm sitting three stools over, trying to drink up some inspiration because, well, I've got a deadline I'm missing, and he just starts telling me how you're his girl and how you ran away because of him, and how it broke your mother's heart."

Ruby felt something in her creak, felt the chasm growing in the facade she had lived behind for years.

The cartoonist looked over at her, took her measure.

She breathed in and breathed out, breathed in and breathed out.

What else did he say? What else? she cried inside. But no word passed her lips.

Mack continued: "Said you'd never want them anywhere close. But they'd had some trouble."

Ruby kept her gaze equal to his.

Trouble. What trouble?

"I asked him where they were staying,'cause I thought it would be a good thing to maybe follow up on, you know," Mack told her. "And the guy started shaking, like tremors. He told me they'd moved into the basement of a boarded-up building down the block from here, one of those condemned tenements down by the park. Squatters, basically."

"And you believed this?" Ruby asked, transforming her panic into incredulity.

"I know it sounds crazy. And at first I thought I was just hooked into some more local color. I mean, the people on the street corners down here tell the best stories you'll ever hear. You take 'em with a bolt of J.D., but you don't take 'em seriously." He paused, looked at her hard: "There was just something about this guy, though. . . ."

There always was, Ruby thought as her mind spun off in too many directions at once. *There always was.*

She blinked, looked down at her hands, tried to conjure the facial tics and hand gestures that would give an impression of weary honesty. "Look, Mack," she said, sighing. "You pull any clip on me ever written and you'll find out that I'm quoted as saying I had an unhappy childhood that I prefer to keep to myself. Period."

"That's kind of ironic, isn't it?" he pointed out. "You getting people to spill their guts on national TV, while you're not telling anybody anything about yourself."

"Maybe. But my life is boring, and it's mine. I'm starting to feel like I live under a microscope. Every time I scurry out into the open, there's a big eye looking down at me. It happens if I pop in or out of a movie theater. It happens if I go out to buy chocolate sorbet." She knew it was a mistake to whine like that, knew it as she said it. But she was just talking to distract him from the effort she was making not to split down the middle, not to fall apart.

He laughed a double-edged laugh. "You're not telling me you go out to buy sorbet, Ruby. I saw you pawing around trying to find cash. I bet you've got a handful of gold cards in there and nothing else." He nodded at her purse.

She grinned at him warmly, rewarding his astuteness, trying to draw him closer. "Which is exactly my point here, Mack," she said. "I can't live my life the way other people do anymore. I have to live by different rules, good and bad. And if I already feel overexposed, you can't blame me for not wanting to go into my own sad past. Can you?"

He shook his head, not in agreement exactly. But in amazement almost. Or frustration. She wasn't sure. She thought it was in her favor.

She leaned across the table. "Which is why you can't

open me up to the kind of speculation that'll come by repeating the wild tales of some hapless drunk."

"You know I could say that you have to put up with a
certain amount of shit to be *Ruby!*" he told her with a sur-
prisingly fierce bitterness. "I could say that you should just
suck it up and pay the price of fame. I could say you
shouldn't be asking me or anybody else for any sympathy."

"You could," she agreed.

They both waited a minute, dueling with silence. All
she had left now was her wile. And her smile. That's all.

She said, "Mack, you're a talented guy, an observer, a
journalist. So what if you do it with jaggedy-hair little cartoon characters? You say something about our culture. You
cut to the marrow, show us who we are, challenge us to get
straight by telling us how stupid we look." She trailed off
for emphasis, angled closer to him as she concluded: "Don't
stoop to talk-show stunts."

He had to respect that, didn't he? Coming from her.
His eyes narrowed and for a while he said nothing, then:
"I'm not going to do anything this week. And maybe I
won't do anything next week or next month. But I'm going
to look into this some more."

"Why would you want to waste your time?"

"Because you came down here today. Because the name
Len Bottom meant enough for you to get on the phone
with me and detour off Fifth Avenue and come down here
today." He aimed the words at her, watched them hit.

She was fiercely steeled against them outwardly even as

they shattered like shrapnel inside her. She bent toward him when she answered: "I came down here today because I'm a fan of yours and wanted to meet you, for one thing. I came down here today because I didn't want you to make a fool of yourself by listening to the kind of parasite that tries every day to eat me alive." She knew how lame she was being. She knew.

A silence stretched between them, taut as the gaze passing across the table. Finally she said, "I could give you example after example."

"Maybe," Mack answered quietly. "But this guy seemed like his heart was broken."

CHAPTER EIGHT

*R*uby's three-hundred-dollar-a-foot shoes had worn blisters on her heels by the time she made it across the street bazaar of St. Mark's Place and then down the last few blocks to Fifth Avenue. Joad was pacing, anger coming off him like heat off asphalt.

"You're late," he said.

"Only ten minutes," she said, collapsing into the backseat. She knew his anger was more about her not telling him what was going on than her being a measly ten minutes late.

"You should've called," he rebuffed her. He was leaning in the door, his eyes searching her for clues. Dear old Joady. He'd never pried. And he couldn't now, though she sensed that he sensed she was in over her head somehow.

"I should've called," she admitted.

"Dag, woman," he said, shaking his head. But a

smile quivered at the edges of his mouth. He shut the door with a muffled click. She slipped off her shoes and rubbed her feet, tried to bring back the feeling in her toes.

Joad climbed into the front and said, "Eden has been ringing in every fifteen minutes. That woman's part clock."

Ruby sighed, and as Joad fired up the car's engine, she picked up the car phone. But she found she couldn't dial. She felt as though her world had gone on tilt. It was all she could do to keep from sliding off into the abyss that had always been waiting there.

Joad was already headed up Sixth Avenue, but she wasn't ready to go back to the Upper East Side. Not yet.

"Joady, could you swing over by Tompkins Square?"

"Tompkins Square Park?" he clarified, giving her another one of those quizzical looks in the mirror.

"That's the one."

Joad backtracked and eventually turned down the street Mack Lewis had mentioned. There was a row of buildings that looked as though they might have gone through the bombing in London. Windows were mostly covered by boards tacked on at skewed angles. Graffiti was tattooed thickly across the bottom third of each building, and there was garbage strewn up what stoops remained. But Ruby knew that it hadn't been explosives but poverty that had blown the glass out of these tenements—hunger and anger and hopelessness. This might not be Shoulderblade. But it looked like home.

"Slower," she called.

She studied the cracked faces of the brownstones, surveyed them for signs of human habitation. They looked deserted to her, and she started to hope that Mack Lewis had met up with an utter crackpot, some crackpot other than her own dad. But just then she saw a flicker behind a basement grate. A child flitted from one window to another, playing like a shadow across them. At first she thought maybe it was only a trick of the light as the late-day sun came in and out of clouds. But then another child appeared, this one in a red shirt. And then they were both gone, gone like rats darting deeper into a garbage heap.

Ruby couldn't look anymore. "Okay," she said. "Get me back uptown."

CHAPTER NINE

$\mathcal{T}$he next morning when the limo was snagged in a rubbernecking backup, horns blaring around them, Ruby saw her own face leering at her from the billboard across the river, and it seemed to goad her, along with the headline that kept unfolding in her imagination: AMERICA'S BIG SISTER LEAVES HER OWN FAMILY OUT IN THE COLD. She still couldn't believe that Mack Lewis was right. But she couldn't persuade herself that he was entirely wrong either. She couldn't. "Trouble," he had said. *What trouble?* She decided that as soon as she could manage it, she was going back downtown.

The show today was about people overthrowing their shrinks. The audience loved it, but the applause didn't reach Ruby. Afterward, as she steamed through the corridor on the way back to her office suite, she was pricked with professional guilt. She knew she needed to stay here. She knew she needed to quash His Own Self right this afternoon and hard. Eden had heard in the ladies' room that the tabloids were all over him like flies on what draws flies: Even the media could smell his mutiny.

So could the Muckety-Mucks, it turned out. Eden filled her in on their plans the minute Ruby regained her desk. They wanted to meet that afternoon to talk about the Page Six item and also to tailor responses to a *New York* magazine query about tensions on the set. They wanted to bring everyone together and have what the most California of them called "team healing."

"Tell them not today," Ruby said when Eden wanted to confirm for three o'clock. Eden looked down at Ruby's schedule on her notepad. Clearly she didn't remember anything that couldn't be juggled. There was Bone, it was true, still trying to get Ruby to focus on the counterproposal he'd received from the network's contract people. But she knew Ruby never minded putting him off. Eden looked back up at Ruby. "What do I say?" she asked.

Ruby paused from throwing videotapes into her bag and getting together the paperwork for tomorrow's show. Nothing but the truth was in her mind, and she couldn't say that. Finally, she shrugged.

Eden gave her an odd look, but of course she would cover, however lamely. It was still her job.

Joad had his Powerbook plugged into the limo's cigarette lighter when Ruby got there. She couldn't tell if he was playing solitaire or working on his screenplay. Either way, she felt bad about interrupting him.

When they pulled up in front of her awning on Fifth Avenue and he opened the door for her (even though she'd told him sixteen thousand times at least that that was not part of his job as far as she was concerned), she gave him the rest of the day off. She saw him shift from one Nike climbing shoe to the other, wanting to ask. But he didn't. It was tempting to tell him, just get it out. She knew he would help her, that he would go with her. But there were some things you had to do alone, even if you were Ruby Maxwell and could afford someone to sculpt your glutes and stretch your shoes and haul you from one borough to the other. There were some things you had to face alone because you should have faced up to them a long time ago. This was hers. "Go shoot some hoops," she told him as she blew him a kiss good-bye. He launched an invisible ball into the air for her, but he watched her turn and go, studied her.

The apartment was filled with sunlight, the way she loved it best, but she didn't pause. She passed through it like a passenger changing planes in an airport. Her destination was someplace else.

She changed into a pair of jeans that she hadn't worn since campaign days. She dug out an old pair of flats. In recent years, she'd only worn heels, which put her eye-level or above the Muckety-Mucks, gave her the stature her insecurities needed. But high heels made her feel hobbled too, in an odd way, like prize horses, which were shod only for the race course and had trouble walking on regular ground. So now the Joan & Davids made her feel strangely agile. She pulled her hair back, twisted it into a French roll, and then she scrubbed her face. In the mirror, she surveyed the results: Without makeup, she didn't look like herself. She'd been twelve years old the last time she had gone out of doors with a naked face.

Pausing to scribble a note to Paul, she remembered how his brow had been drawn into a V over his nose the night before when she had come home late. He had been filled with questions and frustration, and she had been saved only by the arrival of his parents bearing a bottle of Dom Pérignon and all their best wishes for a happy future. Now, she signed the note, "Love, Ru," and then kissed the bottom of the page. But, without lipstick, the gesture did him no good. She left no mark.

Walking east on Eighty-sixth Street, eyes didn't graze her as they usually did. She fell into her old New York habit of keeping her eyes straight ahead, her face matter-of-fact. She was almost at the subway, and nobody had noticed her.

At the subway booth, not knowing how much a token cost anymore, she asked for two, gave the man a twenty-dollar bill, and waited for the change. Then she was on the subway platform, surrounded by smells and sounds and sights she had insulated herself from for years. It made her remember the fear she had felt when she had walked down into the subway system for the first time. But it also put her back in touch with the solid center that had kept her back straight and her chin up and her feet moving one in front of the other, one in front of the other.

The train came, and she stepped on. As it left the station and hurtled through stops of descending street numbers, something in her balked. But, *what trouble*? Okay, she was going. Inexorably, she was going. She had forgotten how fast the subway was, how efficient. Even as she remarked it, she was being forced up the steps, up into the harsh light of Astor Place.

Blinking, she found The Towers to orient herself, then she made her way in the direction of the East River, across St. Mark's. Still, nobody noticed. She wanted to turn back, wanted to dawdle over the books strewn on the sidewalk, anything. She did not want to walk back into Len Bottom's world. Her escape had cost her too much; still, every day, it cost her too much. Her mind could barely touch the memory of that tarpaper-and-tin house on the mountain, where the frayed electrical wires in the kitchen and the leaking refrigerator made it dangerous to walk much less cook, where raindrops fell on her face as she tried to sleep.

"Your dad will take care of it," her mother had told her and told her and told her. And a child believes it, even if there is no evidence, ever. Even if the wires never get bound in black tape and the refrigerator never gets fixed and the roof goes on leaking. That household, like their very existence, was built on a foundation of nothing more solid than their mother's belief in Len Bottom. So what if he had been a smart boy, full of promise? So what if he could "play the fiddle to make the angels break out in song"? What had that ever put on the table? One day, and she knew which day it was, Ruby had woken up and asked herself that. And of course she answered herself, convicted him and convicted her mama for letting it go as terribly far as it had.

As a young man, Len had been sent off to Korea. Other draftees razzed him the way they razzed each other—about the way he said *y'all* and about how much salt he used on his potatoes. But he didn't take it well. He hunched in on himself. Of course he scored off the charts on electronic ability; his daddy's garage had given him that much. And the Army schooled him well, so he was the one the commanding officers wanted when a radio went bad, which was what got him in trouble outside Seoul. He was wounded while bent over a lieutenant's handset, in the few months between when MacArthur got fired and General Ridgeway declared the truce, and he came home to Kentucky bunged up so badly he couldn't work—or believed he couldn't. (Ruby was never sure how dire his physical disabilities were because they never stopped him from tramping around the woods with his coon dogs or shooting target practice at the squirrels he could spot from his front porch La-Z-Boy.)

Lila Chase had been waiting for him when he came home from the war. She was a beauty. Her red hair was spoken of in four counties as being the very red of a bantam's tailfeathers. Which was a compliment. That was about as far as the compliments went for her. She was a Chase, after all. And they were known for having way back moved up into the mountain coves, where they could shoot off their foul mouths and their guns without being bothered. They were also known for their hound dogs and their moonshine. Their children were known for bringing lice to school. Though not Lila. She prided herself on that hair, kept it clean and brushed. It gave her aspirations. She wanted a kitchen with yellow paint on the walls. She wanted stockings that changed colors with the seasons. Years before, when she had heard Len Bottom play the fiddle at a tent revival meeting, she had wanted him, although she had mistaken it at first as the Holy Ghost moving her. Anyway, she had been born again that day, baptized in Shepherd's Creek down below the mill, and Len had paid her no mind. He'd had his draft papers already, was leaving the next day. Probably, he hadn't even thought of her while he was in Korea. But when he got home, she was good enough.

Len cobbled together a house on the land his daddy gave him (gave him despite what they all thought of his choice in brides). For a while, he aggressively pursued nothing at all, let the disability checks go as far as they would. When he got tight for money at the end of a month, he paid the light bill by tinkering with people's cars down at his dad's garage. Bent under the hood, he spewed forth a steady stream of Scripture and vitriol, making the men who came there to loaf and listen say *Amen* as often as he made them blaspheme about the government and the mining companies and Yankee do-gooders. All that spewing was what got him employed for a while. One day, a Ford dealer from up in Ohio broke down on the bridge over Shepherd's Creek, and they towed him into Bottom's, where Len was lying in a puddle of oil under Freddy Jessup's pickup. He was in rare form, citing Scripture and verse about the evils of the goddamn IRS. The barrel-bellied high-roller from Ohio couldn't stop snapping his suspenders in agreement and chuckling. "You're made for the TV," he told Len, and before the night was out, he had made an offer than Len couldn't refuse. Len would go north for a trial run. After that, he went up to Ohio ever so often, pitching cars for the Golden Rule Ford dealership in Wheeler, Ohio. They called him the Rev. L. P. Bottom, and every commercial ended with him saying, "Remember what the Bible says: 'Do unto others as you would have done unto you.' "

Lila loved it, clapping her hands at the sight of him in his black preacher's tie and coat. "Aren't you smart?" she said. His own family scorned it, and of course, Len loathed it most of all, harbored no misunderstanding about what exactly he was doing. He resisted efforts from a regional Ford representative, who wanted him to expand into other northern states. The Ford guy pestered him so much that Len finally came unglued and roughed him up bad enough for an ambulance to get called in: "I'll be damned if I'll make an arse of myself anymore, goddamn hillbilly preacher," Len said when he came home. And that was that. Lila was never going to get yellow paint on her kitchen

walls, never going to get stockings that changed colors with
the seasons. All she was going to get from Len were the
babies. The boys came, one after the other, came right
along with Lila's diminishing expectations: Raphy (after the
great-great-grandfather who came from Scotland), Jasper,
Will, Simon, Cartwright (because of *Bonanza*), Zeke, and
finally, after a lull, Wren (because there was one outside
the window that day he was born). Lila had given up on a
girl and was worn out on boys when Ruby surprised them
all. At Lila's insistence, Len made over their bedroom closet
for the baby girl's room, painting it Pepto-Bismol pink and
hanging a plastic Bambi on the wall that they found out
later Raphy had shoplifted from Ben Franklin's (although
where did they think he got it to begin with?).

Still, even though Ruby caused a stir at first, the place
on the mountain belonged to her brothers. She was nothing
more than their sister—"Sis," as everyone from Raphy to
her mama called her. The boys slept on the screened-and-
shuttered back porch in bunk beds that mounted three
walls. They held belching contests and turned the lights on
and off with their fishing poles. They made sport of insects:
When a mosquito struck, they'd stretch their skin and trap
the snout so the insect would have no choice but to drink
blood until it exploded. Also they picked swollen ticks off
the hounds and kept them in jars until they gave birth to
millions of minuscule ticks, which they tried more than
once to release in Ruby's bed. Some summer nights they
declared a Shiny Heinie and stormed around the yard

smashing fireflies and smearing their phosphorescent tails into glowing streaks all over the tar-paper siding on the house. Ruby stomped and cried at the carnage. Which made the boys snort laughter through their noses like soda pop, which made Len himself rock back and forth and guffaw in his La-Z-Boy, which made Lila snicker too, even as she stroked Ruby's hair in an attempt at comfort, cooing, "Oh, Sis."

They all laughed but Wren, or Runt, as he was known by his brothers and his cousins and therefore most of the kids at school. Wren looked after her. Not in a way that anyone would notice. That would've called down too much torment. He'd just do things to make her feel better. She remembered one Shiny Heinie night when she had gone in to bed, her little room was glowing. It was as though all the stars had come inside to shine on her—all because Wren had filled a Mason jar with lightning bugs and spirited them past the others to set them loose in her room. Dear old Wren. He had been the one to help her get out, the one who had given her the permission she couldn't give herself.

She wished for Wren now. But she was alone, compelled back over the steps she had walked on her last trip to Alphabet City. The streets teemed around her. There was more activity out on the sidewalks here than on the Upper East Side at this time of day. Women sat on stoops.

Children clotted on the corners. Men lurked near the phone booths. She passed through them as though she were invisible. She was beginning to believe she was, until she reached the bar on the corner and looked in. She saw a white face staring back at her, recognized it finally as her own reflection. She made herself look past it and into the dark interior. When her eyes adjusted, she could see the television playing a hockey match. She could see the row of barstools. The corner one was empty.

She turned and walked across the street and deeper into deterioration. She passed the last habitable buildings, and then reached the stretch of condemned properties. Official city stickers proclaimed their dereliction. Her Joan & Davids crunched across tiny vials she thought must've held crack.

There was nothing to do but go house by house. The first building seemed impregnable. She checked where the front door had been. She pried around the basement gate and around the old coal chute. Nothing. She looked over her shoulder. A guy across the street passed with a black garbage bag bulging with what must be bottles and cans. Two women moved down the street with vacant eyes. Nobody even glanced her way.

She was just giving up on the second building when she saw two children disappear into the fourth. She went immediately to where she had seen them last. Again, she tried everything that resembled an entryway. Nothing budged. She stood rooted to the spot, beginning to believe that the children were figments of her hysteria, this time and last. She was starting to believe that this was madness on her part, taking it this far, believing in a stranger's words, a stranger in a bar in a bad part of town.

Then one of the children peered at her from the basement window, looked out through a crack in the plyboard behind the bars. Seeing her, he jerked out of sight. Her stillness had fooled him, faked him out in an eerie form of peekaboo.

Ruby took hold of the bars around the window and called to the children in a loud whisper. "Please," she said. "Can you help me?"

Nothing stirred. She was shaking all over.

She whispered loudly: "I can give you something for it."

She thought she heard the merest brushing of cloth against cloth. She waited, then finally turned to go. She felt the relief of failure.

But the children, both of them, were standing behind her. Their little faces were smudged dark as walnuts, their eyes as hard as that.

"I'm looking for someone," she told them. "Someone who lives around here."

"Nobody lives around here," one of them said. "These places are condemned. Can't you read?"

"A man named Len," she stammered, unnerved by the children's impassivity. "And a woman. Her name is Lila. She has red hair. Like mine."

They squinted up at her. Their lips were held in perfectly straight lines. She had never in her life seen children with such sober control of their expressions. "Where's your camera?" the bigger one asked.

Ruby didn't understand.

"I don't have a camera," she said.

"All you people from the newspapers have cameras."

"Not me," she said. "I'm not from the newspaper."

They just looked up at her, and she just looked down at them, waiting. Finally one looked at the other, then back at her. He held out his hand, palm up.

She reached into the college backpack she had slung over one shoulder, then held out a ten-dollar bill.

The child grabbed it. The other one elbowed him roughly.

The first one looked back up at Ruby again and muttered, "She needs one too."

Ruby handed the other one a bill. She studied the child as she did. It had not occurred to her that this was a little girl, or that the other was a boy. They had seemed like animals to her, sexless at a glance and ruled only by appetite.

But as the girl took the money, Ruby studied her, a new fear choking her. The child didn't meet her eye, didn't say a word. Ruby saw the last bit of chipped polish on the girl's little fingernails. She started to touch her hand, but by then both children had been swallowed up again by the hulking tenement. She bent to follow them through the passageway they had left open. She heard the rustle they made moving away from her across the floor, mere mice. But she had to stop, wait for her eyes to adjust to the blackness.

Then daylight broke at the far end of the room, as the children swung open a door. Its hinges protested, and she heard a television blaring, followed by a woman's voice saying, "Don't leave that door standing open. You know better. That draft'll get us all."

"Mama?" Ruby called. The word was out of her before she even knew she was going to speak. It was out of her past and into the dark musty air, unbidden.

Only the television made a sound, jingling a diaper commercial. Ruby kept walking. She squinted into the bright room from where her mother's voice had come. There were tables made of bricks, the television pulsing on one of them, and a mattress in the corner. She was sitting on it, looking up from a torn romance novel in her lap.

"Is that you . . . Ruby?"

Her mama's hair wasn't red anymore. It was white.

"Oh, Sis," Lila Chase Bottom said. Tears erupted out of her as though someone had thrown a switch. She writhed on the mattress, and it took Ruby a minute to realize that Lila was trying to pull herself up from the floor. Finally, she struggled to her feet and came close, emitting a soft sound, nothing joyous in it, just a steady hum of anguish barely audible.

Ruby couldn't move. She felt her mother's arms go around her, felt the brittle bones of her mother's back as they shuddered in the force of her sorrow.

She pulled away, took two steps back. "Mom," she said finally. "What are you doing here?"

"Come here, Sis. Here, sit down." She reached for her daughter to come to a wired-together chair with peeling paint.

Ruby shook her head. I can't stay, she wanted to say. She didn't think she could bear to stay, could bear what she was feeling in this makeshift room tacked into habitability. But no words came out.

Just then footsteps sounded overhead, and grew big and hollow as they fell on a staircase. A voice from way back in her memory echoed with the footfalls. And then her father was in the room.

"Who's that?" he asked, his voice husky with suspicion.

"Only your girl you come so far to see," Lila said. Just then, the *RUBY!* theme music began to tinkle inanely on the television, a promotional spot. Her father looked at Ruby onscreen and then back to her person.

"Sis?" he asked. Ruby turned her face full to him.

"Hey, Daddy," she said softly.

He looked at her a long minute, and then he allowed, "Well, I'll be damned."

CHAPTER TEN

The little girl seemed part of his shadow at first, moving soundlessly in her worn canvas shoes. Then, still holding his hand, she moved out into the light that fell through the plastic-covered windows. She had strawberry-blond hair. Ruby had never imagined she could be so beautiful.

Tears filled Ruby's eyes. She blinked quickly, looking away from her family. Her mother moved closer and hooked an arm around her waist, squeezed. Ruby had the old, futile urge to push her away.

"Ruby," Lila said softly. "This is Lucie."

Ruby wrested her eyes back to the child. "Hey, Lucie," she said, willing her voice not to crack under the distress she felt.

"Hey," Lucie replied, digging an imaginary hole with the toe of her shoe. She did not look up.

Len's jaw was tight, and he kept a grip on the child's hand. The rough skin on his neck reddened, moving up.

He seemed afraid of Ruby. She had never seen him like this. He seemed to look to his wife for rescue.

Lila said carefully, "Lucie, this is who we came to see."

"My sister, Ruby?" the little girl asked.

Ruby's eyes swung to her mother's for confirmation. Lila nodded, grappling at Ruby with a look that begged her complicity.

Ruby looked back at the child. She felt needled by every emotion and numb at the same time, like part of her had fallen asleep long ago and was now coming back to sensation painfully. She knelt. "Do you have a hug for me?" she asked Lucie.

The child looked up at Len Bottom, not so much for permission as for assurance that no harm would come to her from it. He nodded at her, let a smile escape out of one corner of his mouth. And then Lucie stepped across the room and into Ruby's arms.

Ruby fought herself hard, and won. There were no tears. The last thing she wanted was to frighten this child with a revolt of her own emotions. She concentrated only on the delicate spindliness of Lucie's frame, the fine gloss of her hair. She breathed her in. Then she let her go.

Ruby turned and walked to a far corner of the room. It was as though a stone had been thrown into the center of her life. Stifled sobs rippled through her, breaking. Still, she managed to swallow the tears.

"C'mon, Lucie Goose," Len Bottom said, too loudly.

"Let's go get that table you spotted." There were footsteps, the sound of a door, then only the nattering of canned voices on the television.

"Could you turn that off?" Ruby asked.

Lila switched it off, and Ruby could sense her mother looking at her for what seemed a long time.

"We shouldn't've come," Lila worried, and Ruby suddenly felt, like a chill up her spine, Lila's hand on the nape of her neck. Her mother's palm moved along the French roll. "It'll only make trouble for you, for her. . . ."

Ruby shook her head, lurching away from her mother. "I can't even look at him," she spit out.

Lila's lips quivered. "We wouldn't've come at all . . ."

"What trouble are you in?" Ruby asked.

Her mother looked away, only said, "She kept us together after you. . . . We've raised her as ours. Nobody's told her different, nobody would back home."

Ruby caught her mother's eye, demanded an answer.

"We just don't want to lose her," Lila said. "We couldn't bear that; you know that, don't you?"

Ruby wasn't sure what she knew and what she didn't.

"And we wouldn't've come dragging her up here at all, wouldn't've pulled you into it for anything, but we just can't lose her. We can't."

The words soaked deep enough into Ruby's shocked psyche to make her question what was behind them. "Why?" she asked. "How could you possibly lose her?"

Lila caressed a loose strand of Ruby's hair. "I'd forgotten what a beautiful color it was."

"Mama," Ruby said, pulling away. "How could you
possibly lose her?"

"Oh, the house burned down," Lila said, sighing. "We
woke up one night, and it was filled with smoke. It looked
just like fog, only on the inside, smoldering like. And we
got Lucie and got outside, and the whole thing just went
up, lit up the whole night." She lifted her arm as she said
it, her voice just as languorous as it had always been. Lila
Chase had never raised her voice in anger. In her worst
hours, she had still sounded as though she were singing a
lullaby.

Ruby wanted to shake her. Instead, she asked. "Insurance?"

"You know how it is."

Of course, no insurance. There wouldn't have been
money for it even if there had been the inclination.

"It started in the kitchen," Lila said. "Wouldn't you
know? The neighbors came from miles around. But not a
one of the boys. Not one. Wouldn't lift a finger to help
him. That tells you something, right there."

Ruby didn't understand.

"Why not?"

"Haven't spoke a word to him, not since . . . well, you
know, when you left, that was that. Wren comes and takes
Lucie to play with his girls, sneaks me a little money for
her school shoes and such. And Raphy comes when he's

feelin' flush and takes her for a spin in that pickup of his. But they won't have a thing to do with him, and he's their daddy."

It was too much to take in. "Nobody helped?"

"Help like that we don't need." Lila slumped down on the bed and worried her hands together. "Help like that I wouldn't wish on my worst enemy."

"But what are you doing *here*, Mama?" Ruby looked around the mean little room but she meant here as in New York, as in the middle of her life.

"We had to go somewheres else. That Wren wanted to take her away from us, said he'd take Lucie to raise as his own. He just up and went to the authorities and told his story of what happened with you, dredging up the past when there's no sense in it now, and the social services people were down in town asking questions about how we was living with the house burned down, and so your daddy decided there was nothin' for us to do but leave. Nothin' to keep us there anyway, if they're gonna be that way. Those are our boys. We raised them up, raised them up with nothing but our feeling for them, the feeling a mama and daddy has for their children. We raised them all up, raised you. And now we've got nothin'. Nothin' but that one baby girl. Nothin' to keep us there."

"Nothing?"

"Nothin' but memories that don't do nobody no good, no how."

CHAPTER ELEVEN

*P*aul lunged at Ruby when she walked in the door and told her she needed to talk to that assistant of hers, teach her how to handle people with respect. "Oh, Paul," Ruby said, touching his shoulder, but he was off, pacing around the apartment with a rolled-up *National Geographic* that he kept swatting into his left palm. He had apparently tried to reach her at the office, and Eden had said she was in a meeting, and when Ruby hadn't called back, he had tried again and then again. "She was stonewalling me," Paul fumed.

Ruby was hollowed out by seeing her parents and the little girl, and her only thought was irritation at Eden, at him, at everyone for not somehow stepping back and, magically, giving her the space for the cataclysm to occur. Because it was occurring, that much was sure.

She sighed. The last thing she wanted to deal with

was Paul in a petulant mood, although, really, who could blame him? Two nights ago, she'd told him she would marry him. She'd barely spoken another word to him since.

And she didn't want to say the words she needed to say to him. Not now. Ruby walked past him to their room, shedding clothing as she went. She sighed. *Not now*, she chanted to herself. *Not now. Not now.*

She reached into her armoire for the silk pajamas his mother had given her the first Christmas she'd spent with the Carrigans. At the time, she had been touched by the extravagance, touched to the point of having tears well into her eyes. She took it as a sign of their acceptance. The pajamas were by far the most luxurious thing she'd ever owned, and she turned to them when she needed comfort, when she needed to believe that her life here was real. They were worn thin from comforting her, from proving to her what her own bonuses and investments and bank accounts couldn't.

Paul sat on the bed, watching her button the top, waiting. Sometimes Paul Carrigan could pout. She hadn't seen it often, but just now she thought his privilege was on him like a private-school-boy's uniform.

When her hair was combed out, she went and sat by him, put her hand on his knee. "Look, Paul," she began, then it trailed off in another sigh. Exhaustion was wound around her like gauze. She wanted to tell him the truth, just get it over. Instead, she leaned back into the pillows on the bed. She couldn't set down the burden of her remorse to foist the truth onto Paul, poor Paul.

"I'm so frustrated," he said, striking his knees with the flats of his hands. "I'm just so damned frustrated. My mother is after me all the time about the party and the *Times* and setting a date for the wedding, and I can't get you to even talk about it."

"I'm tired," she said, letting her eyes close.

"Is this about the bad press?" he asked after the silence got loaded with a lot of emotion.

She opened her eyes and looked at him, waved her hand as if the bad press was nothing but a nuisance.

"Ruby, you're making me crazy," he said in a tone rubbed raw with anxiety. "It's like you unbolted one door and slammed another on my fingers." He looked at his long smooth fingers as though he felt the pain there, then shifted his eyes to hers with an uneasiness she'd never seen him display, not in all the years they'd been together. "You're sure there's not someone else?" he asked.

His question penetrated deeper into her than anything he'd yet said. It struck a nerve of the truth and triggered a tremor in her fingers. *Yes*, she answered him inwardly. *Yes, there's this whole gob of people.* But all she said aloud was, "Oh, Paul," just so softly. And then she laughed. She laughed because it was better than crying, which was her only other option at the moment, and when she laughed, he joined her, relief all over him. They giggled together, as though they were once again the best friends they had been all these years, as though they could be again.

He lay down beside her, draped an arm across her waist. He continued laughing even as he launched into how he was sorry but he was just feeling the strain of his mother's enthusiasm: Today, Gracie had taken the liberty of calling her favorite man at Tiffany's and asking him to look for a flawless diamond of a certain size, an appropriate size. Unless they wanted to go to the Winstons, who were family friends, you know, and would do anything for Paul. It was all accomplished with the utmost discretion, of course. "You know how she is," Paul explained with a muzzy chuckle. Paul himself was never one for any kind of fuss; he was also never one to deny his mother any happiness.

"I can't, Paul," Ruby said, suddenly solemn, suddenly not seeing anything amusing about her role in all this and desperately wishing she had just shifted the truth onto his shoulders, had just set herself free. But she hadn't. And she couldn't now. She was too worn out, and besides, something in her was afraid of that freedom she had stepped off into the minute she had stepped onto the Greyhound, the vacuous freedom she had floated in until Paul's voice had risen on the night wind, frightened away her assailants in the park, until that night he had taken her home. Freedom had not been the best thing that had ever happened to her. Maybe it had even been the worst. All these years since, she had relied on Paul to keep her anchored, to keep her

from drifting out again into that terrible, lonely mute freedom. And it wasn't so easy to cut the line that bound him
to her. It wasn't.

"What do you mean, you can't?" Paul teased, kissing
her nose.

She kept her eyes closed.

Paul brushed the hair away from her forehead. And the
tenderness of his touch made the tears come. They forced
themselves out from under her closed eyelids. They ran
down her temples and behind her ears.

"Oh, Ruby," he murmured, pulling her close and holding her in the quiet of their home, where the traffic noise
from down on the avenue seemed nothing more than the
pulse of some benevolent being. The city, the world seemed
like something so good from this apartment, from Paul
Carrigan's vantage point. Everything *down there* seemed
miniature and manageable. It seemed the way things had
seemed when she had climbed the backyard apple tree.

They stayed that way for a long time, his arms around
her, and Ruby savored, as she always had, that serenity he
had given her, that calm harbor of his devotion that had
been hers ever since Liza had gone and he had moved her
into his home. At first, they had camped out here together,
just as he had camped out here alone, sleeping on the mattress on the floor, eating takeout cross-legged on the hard-
woods, reading at night by the light of the overhead
chandelier. And then, just about the time Ruby graduated,
and even though she had already refused his marriage pro-

posal three times, he saw her linger in front of an antique shop's window. He insisted they go in. She found a floor lamp she thought beautiful and a brocade pillow. He bought them. After that, encouraged by his mother, he charged Ruby with furnishing the apartment, with making it as grand as it had been when his own grandmother had brought in the best Upper East Side decorators. Ruby had demurred at first. But she had by that time redecorated herself extensively, and this seemed a much more straightforward effort. There were magazines and books on this subject, at least.

Paul had been so proud of her first move, a bold one. She had purchased a lavish bed that had come down from Danish royalty and been dismantled piece by piece and shipped over by one of the Vanderbilts, who had been in a branch of the family that lost the fortune and the bed with it. Consequently, the bed had found its way to a dealer on Lexington who opened his store by appointment only. He hadn't taken Ruby seriously at first, she thought. She had asked questions about procuring custom-made mattresses that showed her to be an amateur. But then she had done the measurements herself, running a tape up along the four posters and across the friezelike beams that ran under a tapestry ceiling. She had tested the groove work and the fittings. From there, she haggled. When a price was set, Paul simply wrote the check, one with many zeroes in it, and handed it over without comment.

The Carrigans did a lot of tittering about the bed, and

it stood as the lone regal piece of furniture for some months, as though Ruby had satisfied her aspirations with that one marvelous antique. But she was only plotting, carefully planning the pieces that should be arrayed around it, just as a gardener plans the perennials to accent the prized weeping cherry. She read everything from Edith Wharton's *Decoration of Houses* to the auction-house catalogs. She studied the displays at the Met. She got Paul's mother to arrange lunch for her with Martha Stewart. Finally, when Ruby was ready, Gracie happily squired her to Sotheby's and Christie's. They walked up and down Madison, made the occasional foray to Soho or even to Atlantic Avenue in Brooklyn if they heard of the right piece. And Ruby always knew the right piece. Already, it was arranged in this room or that in her imagination, already in its rightful place.

Over the years, Ruby had conceived and choreographed a showplace. But it was never shown. She and Paul lived here alone. If visitors arrived, they were his parents, and they came at their own invitation. The apartment was like a lavish stage set, created at great expense but seen only by the stagehands, who came and went in an empty theater. But it was home, his and hers. And it was as far away from her mama's home as any she could imagine.

"You take your time," Paul was murmuring now, comforting her, and she thought at first that he had seen into her somehow, knew something of her anguish, but then he went on: "You'll get used to people talking, get used to the vultures. This is just too much for you all at once. You're tough, though." He chuckled affectionately. "You were a pit bull on the campaigns. You just aren't used to being attacked personally yet. You'll build up a callus."

He thought her tears were about the Page Six eruption, that's all. He thought they were about the pressures of her fame. His father must have briefed him on the newspaper item. Maybe Gracie had told him that Ruby was feeling fragile. Anyway, he made his assumptions. And they were wrong. He had no idea that Ruby was crying for everything she was about to lose, crying for him. He didn't know that she was crying about a little girl in a torn-apart building in a cruel part of town. He had no idea.

But she let him go on thinking that what was bothering her was nothing more than the inked words on a piece of newsprint that tomorrow a homeless man on Twenty-third Street would dislodge from a trash can, a shred of paper that would blow through traffic and whip out onto the Hudson, where it would settle and drift and dissolve and be nothing at all anymore, nothing.

CHAPTER TWELVE

*H*er room was warm enough for orchids, yet she woke up cold. The radio said it was 28 degrees outside. Spring had veered back into winter. Ruby thought of the wind-sifted building downtown and shuddered.

She had tried to get her father to leave that place. But he had insisted that he had rigged it so they could keep themselves comfortable, heat up a bowl of soup. "Not to worry," he said.

They had kept their voices low, discussing it, after he had brought Lucie home from scavenging an ornate chess table she had noticed set out on the curb with somebody's garbage on East Tenth Street. Probably it had come from Russia, Ruby told the little girl. Some old Russian immigrant had probably played on it every day of his new life here, and when he died his landlord probably set it out on the curb with the rest of the junk he'd had to clean out of the apartment before he could move somebody else in at 15 percent higher rent. She didn't say that part, but she thought it, irritated as she was and stirred up to some height of frustration she hadn't felt in years.

Trying to talk sense into her dad, Ruby had struggled not to let her words flare and attract Lucie's attention from the bottle-cap checker game the little girl was choreographing with the other squatters' children, the ones who had taken Ruby's money and shown her the way in. Ruby tried to be calm talking to Len and Lila.

"Not to worry," Len had said for maybe the fourth time.

"Not to worry?" Ruby had asked incredulously. "This is a squat." She said the word with contempt. "They write articles about the homeless people scrabbling into these places. They're talking about *you*."

Her dad had looked defiant. His smirk hadn't wavered. He'd already bragged how he wasn't like everybody else down here, wasn't the type to sit in a bus station and beg. He had something to offer those who did, though, and so he had established himself as inviolable and necessary in the derelict strip of buildings crawling with cockroaches and human beings with no place else to go. He had siphoned electricity and rigged up hot plates. He had insulated rooms with cardboard and stuffed up rat holes with steel wool he scavenged from the garbage Dumpsters and heaps along the river. He had made the place livable.

Ruby had forged on: "The mayor is talking about razing them, coming in here with the National Guard and just mowing them down."

Still nothing.

"You have to let me put you in a hotel." A hotel. It had even sounded harsh to her, not asking them home with her. But she couldn't have just sprung them on Paul. She had some explaining to do first. "Let me arrange something nice."

"You're not arranging anything, Sis," her father had told her emphatically. "You're only going to draw attention to us, and then where will we be?"

She pointed out that they weren't in Kentucky anymore, that this was New York and nobody here cared a whit where they were or weren't, except when they were trespassing on condemned property, which they all were at the moment. They should go home, back to Shoulderblade. There were programs to help them, housing grants and food programs, and even as she explained she was starting to realize that she was up against not just the Appalachian suspicion of the government and its wile but more intimidatingly, she was up against her father's towering pride and paranoia.

"You shouldn't've come down here," Len kept insisting. "You'll get us found."

"Me?" she had said, and then lost her composure. "You shouldn't drink if you're worrying about getting found." She couldn't even look at him as she said it, the fear was still that much there.

"What's that have to do with anything?" he lashed back.

"You talked in that bar on the corner. Nobody would ever've known you were here otherwise. Me or anybody else."

He rammed her with a hard-eyed look.

"That guy you bellyached to in the bar happens to be a reporter," she explained, "and just happened to call me. Right this minute, he's threatening to expose both of us in his newspaper—you as a squatter and a drunk and me as the granite-hearted daughter who makes nice to the rest of the world and leaves her own family out in the street."

"That round-headed guy with the earring?" Len asked, his black eyes snapping.

"How many others did you tell?"

"I'll have his hide. . . ."

"Sure, you will, and then the prison system will have yours and the child welfare system will have Lucie's and Mama will be out in the cold. What then?" Her voice managed to sound like it belonged to someone calm and reasonable. Not that calm and reason had ever carried any influence with Len Bottom. Maybe stubbornness would.

They had played a game when she was little. "Ready to play Stubborn, Sis?" he'd say at night when he was ready to take off his boots. Her brothers would howl as little Ruby straddled her dad's leg and tried to wrench off his boot. All Len had to do was keep his ankle cocked, and it was impossible for her to free the boot. Even knowing that, she had strained and tugged and wrenched until the cords in her neck felt bruised. Every time, she had struggled until he had unhinged his ankle, then she and the boot had gone flying into the corner. Her brothers held their guts to keep from spilling them in the hilarity of the moment. Ruby just got up off the floor and turned around to get the boot off his other foot. "Look at her," Len had cried in his warped version of pride. "Look at her goin' back for more. That child is tough as an old boot."

Lila Chase Bottom had never been any help to Ruby then, and she hadn't been yesterday down in that pit of a building. In fact, Ruby feared her mother didn't have any fiber left in her at all, not after having been wrenched out of her home. Len Bottom still looked tough and fully charged. His blue eyes glinted coolly out of his red complexion. His shoulders were as square as ever, and his hands were still rough as rawhide gloves. Age made him look more himself, more durable somehow. But it had frayed her mother's delicate beauty. Lila had always had an airy, spun-silk quality. Her beautiful hair, prized for its almost garnet cast, was now gone silver. Naturally slender, she was now alarmingly thin. The pearllike translucence of her skin seemed dusty. From her cigarettes, she had a cough that seemed bigger than she was.

"I'll find you a nice place," Ruby had said, as though it were settled.

It wasn't. "You try messing with me, Sis, and we'll evaporate like raindrops in August. Depend on it." His jaw was locked on his convictions. He'd led her to misery with his convictions.

Ruby had never known how to get him to turn loose of that anklebone, never known how to get him to turn loose of even one of his bad ideas or to turn loose of her.

"Nobody can take her away from us," Ruby had said at last. She had said it with slow and steady emphasis. "She's *my* daughter."

Lila's eyes had darted nervously across the room to see if the little girl had caught Ruby's words. Len had clenched his fists. But the child hadn't looked up from her game board. "You put that back," they heard her tell the little boy saucily, her hands on her little hips. "You put that right back."

Len had leveled his eyes onto Ruby's, had spoken low and cut deep. "You ran out on her," he said. "You abandoned any rights you ever had. And they sure as hell can take her away from us with their lies. I'd like to string that Wren up like I shoulda done to them all when they were boys, taught them a little respect. But don't you go talkin' big to me. You ran out on her, ran out on me, ran out on your mama."

She had felt as though he were head-butting her with words. She had felt as though all the air had been knocked out of her hard, like she would never get another breath worked into her empty lungs.

Len had shaken his head in disgust then, not just for her. "This is what I get for going off half-cocked," he said, more to himself than to either of the women who stood there watching him. "I saw your picture on the *TV Guide*, and I headed to it like a lighthouse. You're not supposed to head toward the lighthouse, Sis. There lie the rocks." He shook his head again, this time as if to shake off all the things that dogged him, all the things he could've changed if his back hadn't been broken in the war, and his spirit, everything he could have changed but couldn't now. "I thought you must be rich. I thought you might feel you owed something to us after ditching us."

His stony eyes had found hers again. She felt sore from them by now, battered by everything he'd said and by his looks that said even meaner things.

"That's all you want from me?" she had said. "Money?"

"That's all. Then we'll be as gone to you as you've been to us all these years past."

"Len," Lila had chastened him, moving closer to Ruby as if she could absorb some of the blow. She took Ruby's arm: "Don't you believe that tone in his voice, Sis. He's grieved over you, over what he did. He didn't come after your money."

Len's eyes hadn't softened, though.

Ruby had torn open her backpack. She had spilled out money all over the floor, hundred-dollar bills she'd carefully brought. Because hadn't she lived long enough with the Carrigans, long enough in New York to think that money was the answer? To think that money could save them all? Because wasn't money all she had been for sure willing to offer of herself there in that falling-down tenement? Wasn't that all?

"Take it," she had said. "I'll get you more."

The children had hushed over their game board. They were watching the money flutter to the floor. Ruby could tell the little boy wanted to pounce on it. But his eyes kept scuttling between the paper bills and the towering fury coiled in Len Bottom's fists, and so he had hung back.

It was Lucie who had arrested Ruby. The girl's skin had blanched, except for two glowing pink spots on her cheeks, and she was absolutely still. Ruby had wanted to take the child in her arms and run, as she had in all the dreams she'd ever had about the baby she'd left sleeping in a box in the closet bedroom up at Shoulderblade. But she saw Lucie looking not to her for reassurance, but to Lila, to the woman who had been there when she cried out in the night and who had taken her to school the first day and been at home that night. Lucie wasn't looking at Ruby. Lucie didn't seem to know she was even there.

$\mathcal{T}$he last thing Ruby wanted to do was go to work, and that's what she told Joad when he tucked her into the backseat.

"You read the *Post* already, huh?" he said.

"Oh, crud no," she said. "Not more?"

"Oops," he said, ducking his head in shame to be the messenger.

She looked out the window and wished she could slip anonymously into the stream of people headed toward the Lexington line, wished that she could go down into the subway with them and ride to a station where she got off every day and stopped at a newsstand where she knew the guy's name and bought a pack of Pep-O-Mint Lifesavers and a newspaper that never once mentioned her name and that she stepped into an elevator and went up twenty floors to a little tucked-away office where every day she did her job and ate her sack lunch, a place where every two weeks she got her paycheck and collected no grief with it. She wished.

Joad was handing back a videotape. "Take it," he said. "It's gonna solve all your problems."

She snorted.

"Pop it in the machine, RubyDoo," he instructed.

She did. It was Geraldo. He had a bunch of kids on talking about how they serially deflowered virgins. It was disgusting.

"What?" she asked Joad. "Same ol' slime."

"Recognize anyone?"

And all of a sudden she did. "Wasn't that kid gay and checking his nose hairs in my Green Room?"

"Shazam," said Joad.

She decided it was a good thing she'd been brought up playing a game called Stubborn. It had made her strong, and today she would have to be.

"You kick some butt," Joad told her with a wink as she got out of the car and brushed past the autograph hounds and into the atrium and up the elevator to a showdown.

She backed herself up first, called accounting and investigated what checks went where. She requested transcripts of preliminary guest interviews. And then she went looking for Trev, sat down in his office, and watched him chew his pencil and deny he had anything to do with the leaks to Page Six.

"Oh, I know that," she told him. "You'd be too afraid of calling attention to the bald, fat, horrendous fact that you've been paying guests to appear on my show."

She told him how she'd found him out and informed him that if he'd done it with someone who actually made it onto live air, then he was gone and his reputation with him.

"Don't . . ." he stammered.

"Don't yourself," she said, standing to leave. "And another thing, Trev. Find out who did leak the stuff to Page Six."

"Me?"

"Yeah, you. Birds of a feather."

It occurred to her as she was walking back to her office that maybe Eden had rubbed off a little on her after all.

Éden got her the number for the Stanhope, and Ruby made the call herself. The Stanhope was the closest hotel to her apartment. If she installed her family there, she could catch odd minutes with them until she got everything straightened out with Paul. Even the thought of him pinched her hard.

She rang the hotel. The efficient clerk said they were fully booked. Ruby said check again with the Man in Charge, please. The clerk confirmed again. Ruby requested a word with the Man in Charge, who was on the line after she waited on hold with Muzak for some minutes. He began his apologies, and she swallowed hard, pushing down her pride and her fears and toting up her privilege. She said, "This is Ruby Maxwell, and I need a suite at your hotel." The Man in Charge looked into things again. This time, he found something. Maybe they'd just lost the reservation of some poor Japanese businessman, who knew? Anyway, she asked for an entrance that suited her need for privacy and was assured that it would not be elegant but it would be at her disposal. "Don't worry about a thing, madame," he said.

Eden came in. "Word is you chewed on His Own Self?" she said with a grin.

"Who says?"

"My sources in le john, of course."

"Did I ever," Ruby admitted.

"You know who he leaked to?" Eden asked, surprised.

"No, I know why he didn't leak anything."

"He didn't?" Eden went wide-eyed.

"Uh-uh." Ruby lifted an enigmatic eyebrow.

Eden leaned closer for details.

"Can't tell," Ruby said.

Eden swayed back, looking hurt. "Gossip is a perk of my job, remember?" The subtext of that one clanged.

Ruby laughed to dispel the tension. Eden bent close again.

"Someone may have been paying people to come on the show," Ruby said through theatrically tight lips.

"Do tell," Eden said, pulling up a chair.

Ruby swept an imaginary zipper across her lips and threw away the key. They both laughed, then Eden handed her a list of the calls she had held. Ruby scanned them. Mack Lewis's name punched right out at her, knocked her down a notch.

"Could you keep everybody out of here for a few minutes?" she asked Eden.

"Sure," her assistant said. "Why?"

Ruby looked up at her, manufactured an amused look that would not have won any Emmys. "Because . . ." she said, mysteriously.

Eden held up both hands and backed out of the room. She closed the door behind her.

Ruby pecked in the numbers. The phone rang so long she was certain a machine was going to pick up, but as her hope seeped almost entirely away, he answered.

"Mack Lewis," she sang out, as though his were the dearest voice in all the world to her, as though she were so, so, *so* glad to be hearing from him again. "This is Ruby."

"Ruby Blossom Bottom?" he asked.

CHAPTER THIRTEEN

*T*oad took her home. Ruby went up, changed, and dashed off a vague note for Paul riffing something about a dress-fitting for the engagement brunch. Then she hailed a taxi.

Mack Lewis had done just what she'd told him to. He'd pulled all the press clips ever done on her. Of course, they alluded only elliptically to her childhood. She'd never given anything away. In fact, for her own reference, she had a whole make-believe past that she'd referred to if the subject ever needed dancing around, a daydream that involved an old family plantation in Georgia and an avenue of water oaks. Never had she mentioned Kentucky. There was not one word in all those newspaper stories about Shoulderblade or the Bottoms or a Greyhound bus. But Barnard was all over them.

And once Lewis was at Barnard, there was a pretty convincing paper trail of letters and applications and thank-you notes, all signed with that tightly wound, hopeful little coil of a signature: Ruby Blossom Bottom.

All he'd had to do was find the right, ambitious little journalism hound to help him out, snoop around in confidential files during work-study time. He'd had no trouble with that part, she was sure, not with his hip downtown reputation, which was bound to play well on campus. With very little effort, she was sure, Mack Lewis had pretty much confirmed what he'd already heard from that weepy old guy sitting at the corner barstool. Now, he was loaded with his own little ready-for-the-talk-show-circuit scoop.

In her imagination, it was already Wednesday: All those big, blocky panel trucks rolled down the streets of Manhattan and out into the boroughs. The stacks of freshly printed *Voices* got plunked down out front of the newsstands. Hands settled on them, picked them up. They got carried down into subways and up into office skyscrapers. They got laid open on desks, thumbed through. And of course everybody read the cartoons first. And there she would be, America's beloved sister mutated into a spiky-haired caricature with a dark secret. And there would be her dad, mad and soggy-eyed and scared as all hell.

If Ruby didn't get to her dad before Mack Lewis did, she didn't know what he would do. She just knew she didn't want to find out. It shamed her, but she wasn't sure if she was running so hard to find her family more because she didn't want her dad to kill somebody at the *Voice* or more because she couldn't stand to have them out in the cold anymore. She looked at the wintery rain that was pelting the taxi and hoped that it was because she wanted them safe, especially the little girl. No, of that she was sure: She wanted that little girl safe. She did.

Out the streaming window, she could see that the traffic lights were reflected in the street like spilled paint. The cabbie, a friendly guy with a Pakistani singsong accent, kept craning over his shoulder to look at her. Every conversational spark he struck, she doused. She kept resolutely staring out the window, her hand held along one side of her face, blocking her profile. Fortunately, it was dark already.

"You know they blame us for everything," the driver was saying from the front seat. "They say we are the criminals, the cabbies. Can you believe?" He scoffed forcibly. "We're the workingmen of this city. We keep it moving."

She hummed some sort of answer.

"You don't believe me? Ask the tourists. They're scared to death of us. Everyone tells them, Watch the cabbies."

Ruby shook her head, as if in mutual disgust.

"Those people don't understand New York," he was saying. "This is the greatest city on earth, the most famous. And you know what it's famous for—murders and muggings and rapes. Someone gets their throat slashed in Central Park, I tell you, it's on the television sets in the Khyber Pass. I tell you."

She nodded.

"But you have to take the good with the bad," he said. "It's like your hand. . . ." He held up his hand, fingers splayed. "Your fingers are not all equal. But you wouldn't cut any of them off." He laughed, pleased with his philosophizing. "And that's the way with this city—you have to take the good with the bad, we're all of us here."

She nodded and willed the light to turn green. It did, and the cab surged forward and kept going as every light on Second Avenue turned green at their approach, pushing them downtown like some kind of traffic peristalsis.

He couldn't believe she wanted to disembark at Tompkins Square Park. Not to waste a second, she gave him a fifty, told him to keep the change. He got out of the cab and followed her. "Ma'am," he said. "You think you gave me a twenty but this is a fifty."

"Keep it," she whispered harshly.

"It's a fifty," he called again, waving it. Cars were backed up behind his cab in the narrow street, honking. People looked up from under their rain-slick umbrellas.

"Keep it," she yelled over her shoulder. She ran into someone hard as she turned to run toward the blasted-out building where her family was bunkered. It was a tall man whose face was pulled deep back into the gloom of his hood. She thought of the crack vials that had crunched underfoot on her first visit.

"Watch it, bitch!" he roared. And then he cursed at her and his fate in general.

"Sorry," she muttered, trying to keep her face in the shadows of the shawl she had thrown over her head and shoulders. She brushed past him as he hung in the green haze of streetlight, loitering, his profanities venting out into the wet night like toxic fume.

Ruby ducked into the black shadow of the building, hoping it was the right one. The disguised door swung after a few tries. The interior was impenetrably dark, and the dankness was worse than before, choking, even. By feel, she headed in the direction of the door. But when she found it, there was no light behind it.

Only the plastic-shielded windows let in enough of the city brightness for her to make out that no one was there. Every quilt was gone, every piece of clothing. The television was missing. Lucie's ornate chessboard table was not there. Only the mattress on the floor remained.

She was too late.

"Dad," she cried into the night. Her voice echoed ominously in the deserted building. She heard rodent feet move over her head. "Don't," she pleaded. "Please don't."

And even as she said it, she realized with true anguish why she had come. She knew suddenly and all through her body that she'd lost Lucie again and that she couldn't bear that. She knew that she couldn't bear it and, horribly, that she had no choice. She was too late.

Chapter Fourteen

Outside, the rain was falling so hard each drop seemed to detonate as it struck the pavement. The wind blew great metallic sheets of it down the street. She hesitated in the doorway, getting her bearings, planning which way to turn. It had been years since she had tried to get a cab in the rain.

The minute she emerged from the dark of the stoop, she saw men hunched under the streetlight. And they saw her. "See," cried the man she had rammed into earlier. "I told you she went into that one."

The second man had his shoulders rounded against the dampness, but he straightened at the sight of her, stared hard. "Ruby Maxwell?" he called, taking a step. The rest of his words were swallowed whole in a howling blast of wind.

She bolted. She ran to the end of the block and crossed the street against the light. Tires grabbed for traction on the wet pavement, screeched in the effort. The cars missed her. Their drivers cursed out the windows. And she just kept moving.

At Astor Place, she saw a man getting out of a cab on the corner just ahead. She put up her arm and yelled for it. The cabbie waited grudgingly. He didn't say a word as she gave him the address, as he gunned the car away from the curb. He was surly and silent. She thanked heaven for small favors.

Her heart pounded all the way uptown, and her mind spun off its own walls, ricocheting erratically. She couldn't go home, couldn't deal with Paul. Not yet. Instead, she went to the Stanhope's side entrance, past the garbage bins. It wasn't the most elegant way to enter, but it was private. The security guard who let her in was the only person she encountered on her way up to the suite. Once there, she didn't turn on any lights. She could see by what reflected off the Metropolitan Museum, just up and across the street.

In the bathroom, she took off her clothes, toweled off her hair, and wrapped herself in the thick robe hanging on the door. She drifted through the rooms, looking at the bed where her parents should've spent this foul night. She sat on the bed that would have been Lucie's. She lay back on its pillows and felt the oppression of sorrow that she remembered from years ago, felt again what she had tried to flee. She felt her helplessness and her loss and her old longing for Dewey, for his rescue.

"Oh, Dewey," she said into the darkness. "What am I supposed to do now?"

No answer came. He was lost to her. Len and his shotgun had seen to that. She would never hear Dewey's voice in comfort again. Instead, she got only the sounds of the city throbbing and moaning to itself. She got only the memory of that one summer of her life, that one span of happiness when she had lived inside the secret of their love. Dewey wasn't that much older than she. He was still young enough to believe in his own power to change hard lives. But he was, after all, her teacher, and his loving her would have provoked the school board to put an indelible black mark on his reputation. Not to mention what it would've provoked Len Bottom to doing.

But Ruby couldn't stay away from Dewey, and she guessed he couldn't find it in himself to ask it of her. So she took the job at the Dairy Queen and told her mama she worked more hours than she did. She stayed after school for responsibilities that didn't exist. She went running around with Liza at night, but didn't. Every stolen moment, she was with Dewey.

That summer, they lived those moments mostly in the dark. At dusk, they'd picnic out behind the screen of the lilac bushes, whispering to each other, eating the bread he baked and the cheese his grandma still made at the farm in Laurel County. There was a blue moon that June, and inside the cottage, they would move from room to room by the moonlight that fell through the mullioned-glass panes or by the starlight on moonless nights or by the sudden blue illumination of lightning, flashing when she was standing with her hand on one post of his rocking chair and he with his hand on the other, flashing again when she was in his arms. Electric light would've betrayed them, and anyway, they didn't need it: They listened. If it rained, they'd sit in the rocking love seat in his front parlor and listen to what the raindrops said on the tin roof of the porch. Or they'd listen to the insects rhapsodizing about the July heat. Or Dewey would put on the jazz records that clicked and popped like a winter fire but played songs cool as the breeze that came through the windows and lifted the curtains like ghosts who watched over them as they lay in the bed under the quilt some great-grandmother had made a long time ago. They listened to the rustle of the worn-cotton sheets against their skin, and the whispering of her skin against his, the beating of his heart against hers. They listened to each other, and not at all to reason.

CHAPTER FIFTEEN

$\mathcal{R}$uby opened her eyes, tried to remember where she was. She sat up as suddenly as the realization came: She'd fallen asleep at the Stanhope. She checked the window. It was still nighttime.

Her mind scrabbled back, trying to recall what it was that she had told Paul in the note. Whatever it was, it wasn't enough. It couldn't cover half the night.

Four-twenty-eight, the nighttable clock read. She rushed into her clothes, which were still damp. They felt stiff on her, unfamiliar. It was as though she had stepped into somebody else's life.

She covered the blocks home swiftly, her head bent under the rain, her shoulders plowing against the wind. Her doorman was dozing. He nodded drowsily at her, too sleepy to care where she'd been until this hour.

In the penthouse, the crystal chandeliers were blazing. Every stained-glass table lamp was turned on, every floor torchère. Paul was sitting in the corner of the couch, his spine straight, his shoulders squared. When she closed the door behind her, he stood. He began going to every light and turning each of them off. Then, he went into the bedroom. He was in bed with his back to her when she got there.

"Paul?" she said. He snapped off his bedside light.

She lay there the rest of the night, not sleeping. In the morning, Paul rose early. With relief, she heard him leave the apartment. It was easier that way. The truth had taken hold of her now, and it made no room for Paul, no room for procrastinating. She would have to take her fate off hold. She would have to tell Paul, couldn't go on torturing him with her silence. But not now. He had spared her that, at least.

A cold wind ran down Fifth Avenue like a torrent of icy water. She ducked into the car, shivering and tucking her shawl around her more closely. Her little daughter was being swept along in that current. Her shivering deepened into a chill at the thought.

Joad handed back her Starbucks. It didn't warm her. Nothing could. Or so she thought until Joad broke the news. Then she went hot all over. Now Page Six had an item insinuating that actors were being paid to appear on *RUBY!*

She felt her skin turn red. The article didn't blame it on Trev Jones. It pointed its sneaky little implications at

Ruby, accused her of being desperate to make the show burn nationwide as it had in the tri-states. It said that her trademark sweetness was looking more and more saccharine.

"Two words," Joad said, scanning her face in the rearview mirror. "Skewer him."

"I'm not sure it's him," she said. "Why would he do it?"

"Who else is gonna do it, Ruby?"

Her mind groped. It could be someone in accounting, someone curious about why Ruby had wanted the paperwork, someone who could look at this check here and that check there and add it up the same as Ruby had done. But why do it in a way that hurt her? Maybe it was someone in Trev's team who was disgruntled with him. Lord knows that was no stretch. Or maybe Joad was right: It could be Trev himself, deftly shifting the blame onto her.

"I don't know," Ruby said aloud.

She felt siphoned dry by last night, by the memories and the lack of sleep. She could only look out the window of the car and move into the office as though sleepwalking and then stand in the windows of her suite, looking out at the comings and goings down in the studio lot. She wasn't even aware of Eden coming to stand by her side. The young woman touched her shoulder. "You okay?" she said. "Can I get you anything?"

Eden had obviously seen Page Six.

Ruby shook her head.

Eden brought her an Evian and an Advil anyway, then directed Ruby in to Fritz, who asked for praise of spectacle frames number 208 and ran his fingers through her hair and talked sweet nothings and then pointed her in the direction of her next responsibility.

On the way into the Green Room, Ruby detoured into the staff rest room that said FEMMES on it. She needed a minute, and no one would think to look for her there. There were getting to be fewer and fewer places for her to hide and more times when she wanted to. She sighed, touched the undereye bags visible even through Fritz's puttied-on makeup, then secluded herself in a stall to sit down and hold her breath. She had to starve the fire raging inside her, smother it so she could get through the show.

The outer door of the rest room opened, and the sounds of the office drifted in, then disappeared as the door swung shut. Footsteps crossed the tiles. The door opened again; more footsteps followed.

"Is that you?" Ruby heard a young woman's voice call from one stall to another.

"It's me," a second girl answered. It was Eden. "How'd you know?"

"The boots. I noticed them when you were getting her Evian. Slammin'."

"Eighth Street. Twenty-nine bucks, can you believe it?"

"Better than Maud Frizons any day," the other woman snickered.

"She's wearing her own damn shoes today, Miss Goody Too-Tight Shoes." The girls laughed in perfect sneering unison.

As her heart sunk, Ruby lifted her feet to avoid under-the-stall-door detection.

"Is she still sleeping with Ethan?" the other woman asked conspiratorially.

Eden snorted "She was never sleeping with Ethan."

"I read it in *People*. Her office said no comment."

"She told me not to deny it," Eden said. "Good for her image. Told *Entertainment Weekly* the same thing."

"Maybe she's gay."

"Are you kidding? That woman is asexual, a complete emotional quadriplegic. Doesn't feel a thing below her pretty face."

The toilets flushed one after the other. Then the water sluiced into the marble sinks. Ruby heard them unzipping their purses, heard the combs snapping through their hair, heard them zipping their purses again.

"She's ant bait, if you ask me," Eden blasphemed. "She just puts on that sweetie-hon-sugar voice and gets everyone to come do her bidding. And then she just uses you up. But what goes around . . ."

". . . comes around."

They laughed again as the door swung closed behind them.

Ruby brought her feet back down to the floor.

Chapter Sixteen

*T*hree phone lines were ringing when she closed her office door after the show. She answered the first. It was Gracie.

"I'm sorry, Gracie, but I can't talk now. I can't," she said and hung up. The last thing she could think of at this moment was the party Gracie was planning for tomorrow, the party for an engagement that wasn't, in celebration of a wedding that was never going to be. As she answered the next line, she wondered, Where was Eden, anyway?

"Ruby Maxwell," she said into the phone receiver.

"Ruby?"

"Mama? Where are you?"

Her mother's voice was compressed between a screech of tires, a waning siren. It sounded unequal to the work of making its way from whatever phone booth on whatever street corner to Ruby's ear: "He doesn't want you to know."

Ruby quizzed her mother, who hedged at first, then told what she could. Her teeth were chattering, that much Ruby knew for sure.

"You stay there," Ruby said, after she had pried loose the details. "Stay."

Ruby never answered the third phone line. It was still clicking persistently as she swung out her door into the sudden silence of the staffers, who stood in clots around the office, and then on out into the raw wind, where Joad was dribbling a basketball to amuse himself and the security guys. He was surprised to see her.

"Eden didn't call," he told her, hurrying to open the door for her.

"Nope," Ruby confirmed. "I'm in a rush, rush, rush."

He revved the engine. "You okay?" he asked.

"I don't know, Joady. I don't know anymore."

He made for Manhattan. And all the while, she was in the backseat knowing that he was at the wheel waiting for her to explain. But how could she?

Lila had told her that the day before, Len Bottom had moved them to the upper story of the condemned brownstone, squeezed them behind a false wall he'd made there. What madness! Ruby fumed. Did he think this was some war game?

It was all because of Mack Lewis. The cartoonist had come snooping around the day before, had almost found the right door. Len had been watching him the whole time from the parlor-floor window.

Her father would never have consented to calling Ruby back into things. He had even made them all stay absolutely still when Ruby had come looking for them the night before. They had heard her voice rising from below like smoke and escaping up through the cracked rafters. Her mother tried to get up, but Len had held her so hard his handprint was still on her arm the next morning.

But the night had only tempered Lila's resolve. The wind had keened through the old building, and Lucie had shivered against her grandmother's ribs long after dawn had come. She was hot to the touch. Lila Chase Bottom was not going to conspire with her husband to the detriment of her daughter, to the detriment of this little granddaughter. Not again, she wasn't.

She told him she was going to the drugstore for medicine. Len said he would go. She said he wouldn't know cough syrup from moonshine, and especially for a child. And so he let her go. It was the first time she had been out alone in thirty years maybe, and not in Zachariah County but in the East Village. She waited for a kid in low-slung pants and a backward cap to finish using the phone. She waited though he slid her malevolent glances over his shoulder for standing too close. But she didn't back off. She stood there clutching the card Ruby had slipped her with the phone numbers on it, the one for home, the one for the office, the one for the car, and the one that was always with Ruby though not always turned on. She waited until she could drop her own quarter in the slot, then she dialed Ruby at work.

Ruby noticed that the limo had made it all the way downtown. She told Joad where to turn.

"That place again?" he said, bouncing an inquiring look off the rearview mirror.

"My family's there, okay?" she said. "They're in trouble, Joady, and it's a long, long story. Could you keep the engine running? I'm going to go in and come right back out with them."

Immediately after the car turned into the side street, though, she saw it was going to be harder than she had thought. There were more people on the street than she had expected. She wished for darkness but had no choice now.

She dashed out of the car, heard someone say, "There she is." Footfalls pounded the concrete hard, and they drove Ruby ahead of them faster. She ducked into the mildewed darkness under the brownstone stoop, pulled the door closed behind her.

"Mama?" she called.

"We're here, Sis." The voice was right in front of her face, but she couldn't see them with her sun-stunned eyes.

"There's a reporter out there. He's got a photographer with him," her father said angrily. "Worse than buzzards." He had a rabid-skunk look in his eye. She worried that he had been drinking, and then smelled it on his breath.

"Yeah, well," she said. "There's nothing we can do about that now."

Her mother's arms were full of quilts and pillows. Her father swung his old knapsack over his shoulder and picked up the chessboard Lucie had found on the street and brought home as her own. Ruby looked at it, skeptical about slipping it out as inconspicuously as she hoped they could all slip out, but her father shrugged and skipped a look off the little girl standing at his side. Ruby looked down at Lucie.

"I'm going to carry you," she told her.

"These are my fast tennis shoes," Lucie replied, holding up a blue canvas sneaker with a lady bug embroidered on the toe. "I can run faster than fast."

"I'm sure you can. But we're gonna fly."

And they did, but not so swiftly that the camera couldn't catch them in their flight. Ruby heard the automatic film advancer on the camera running full bore. A man stayed shoulder-to-shoulder with her, asking questions, and she wondered how he had found out, wondered who had tipped him off. She didn't give him the satisfaction of hearing her utter a single word.

The back door of the limo was open for them. Her mother slid in, then her father. Ruby clambered in with Lucie, a camera in the child's face the whole time. When Lucie shifted off her lap onto the seat, Ruby turned back to slam the door shut, and Joad revved the engine. "Ruby," the man said, as the photographer shot over his shoulder.

"Is this your child? Is this a secret you've never told?"

She looked at him for the first time, looked into his dromedary-like face, into his heavy-lidded eyes, and she decided she had learned more than a thing or two from Eden and learned it the hard way: She aimed for where it would hurt him most, kicked hard. He fell back. The door slammed. And Joad sped off.

CHAPTER SEVENTEEN

*H*er parents were shrinking in the luxurious hotel room. The bravado had blown out of her father, and, deflated, he was sitting uncomfortably in the corner of a damask couch. Her mother was standing dazed at the window, holding on to the curtain as if for anchor, singing old hymns to herself. "*Shall we gather at the river, the beautiful, beautiful river . . .*" Lucie, hopping like a little grasshopper, went from Len's knee to take hold of Lila's pinky. She swung Lila's hand, and Lila looked down into her upturned face and laid a hand on the girl's forehead. "Her fever's down," she said, even as Lucie wiggled her nose up and sniffled ostentatiously.

"Good," Ruby said, darting a look at her father. How could he have kept the child in that sieve of a brownstone?

But if Len felt any remorse, he didn't show it. He didn't show anything but raw nerves. And Lucie seemed to sense it—his nervousness and Lila's fear and Ruby's awkwardness. As Lucie moved back to Len's knee and bounced on it like a pony, though she was too big for that, really, it seemed to Ruby that the child was trying to absorb all the foreign feelings she sensed around her, trying to absorb them and make them go away. Children had guile that way, knew enough of their own powers always to be trying to use them. Ruby herself remembered singing and dancing and hanging upside down from a branch of the apple tree, just trying to distract the grown-ups from whatever it was that had drawn their faces into masks she didn't recognize. She remembered her brothers jumping off the shed roof and hobbling the hound and bloodying each other's noses just trying to get their mama and dad to look anyway but *that way*. Poor Lucie. How often had she tried to run fast enough, fall hard enough, sneeze loud enough to change them? How often had she tried to grow big enough to seal up the cracks in Lila and Len?

And even as she thought it, even as the thought went through Ruby's mind, she got the flash of clarity that seared her: She could not blame Len and Lila for not being any stronger than they had ever been, couldn't blame them for making this child frantic to make them feel happier. It was Ruby's fault that Lucie was a little lightning rod for all the pain in this room, for all the pain left behind back at Shoulderblade, and for all the pain uncovered at Tompkins

Square and now at the Stanhope Hotel. Ruby had left her to that. It was Ruby's fault. Nobody else's. Even the first time Ruby had held Lucie, the newborn had looked at her with eyes that shone with hard and pure hunger, every bit as voracious as Lila. Ruby had looked at that tiny bud-fisted infant, begging with those purple eyes, expecting too much, needing more than Ruby had it in her to give, and Ruby's first words to her had been, "Oh, no, little baby grape-eyes." Ruby had cooed it to her as a lullaby. "Oh, no, no, no . . ."

Lucie went up on her tiptoes now and leaned into the window to look at the waterfall of steps coming down from the Metropolitan. It was pure springtime out there now, a bright blue afternoon with breezes that sputtered in the colored flags draped on the museum. The trees with their new leaves looked like ruffled chartreuse carnations, flowers for picking. "Can you climb them?" she whispered to Lila.

"Better not," Lila said.

"Are you a tree climber?" Ruby asked the child, a little too loudly, a little too eagerly.

Lucie stood on the side of her foot, looked over her shoulder and nodded.

Ruby said, "I used to climb that apple tree in the back-yard at home."

"I know," Lucie said.

"How do you know?" Ruby teased her.

"Wren told me. He remembers."

Bless his good heart. Of course Wren would've talked about her to Lucie, tried to keep some sense of her alive to the girl. Even if Ruby herself had done nothing more than send him money for the little girl, anonymous money orders once a month, which had grown over the years from twenty dollars to thousands.

"Daddy put me a treehouse in that one," Lucie said, more to the window than to Ruby.

Len shrugged, confirming. "I tacked up a few boards."

"It's my secret place, where nobody goes but me."

And Ruby's heart rushed to Lucie, though Ruby herself stayed in the brocade chair by the door, her arms folded across her waist, holding herself. Her heart rushed to the child and told her she knew what it was to need a secret place up there on the mountain at Shoulderblade and that she was sorry, so sorry, to have left Lucie that need, to have bequeathed it to her like an heirloom quilt, to have passed it down along with the red hair. She was sorry.

Len jerked up out of the couch and paced around the room. "You'd think they'd have a drink somewhere here. Hospitality-like," he said.

"You'd think," Ruby echoed, feeling the minibar key tucked away in the silk pocket of her shirt, safe from him.

Lila sang another verse of "The Lily of the Valley,"

and Len sat back down hard, turned the television's remote control over and over in his hands, studying how it
was put together. Finally, he collapsed back against the
couch, grunted. Ruby swallowed hard. Lucie traced the
outline of a tree on the closed window. And silence
crept out of the corners of the room to stand between
them all.

CHAPTER EIGHTEEN

She stayed the night. It was easier than going home to Paul. She didn't even call him. It was mean, she knew. But she couldn't think a straight line to him, couldn't think what she needed to say to him, pure and simple, when every thought got deflected off her mama and her daddy and her little girl. She just couldn't.

Early in the morning, while everyone else slept, she got up and put back on the same clothes from yesterday, because it was her only choice, and she slipped out of the building. She crossed the street, walked up past the museum and into the park. She had to go home, but she would go this way, with the green around her, the trees: celebrity be damned.

Always, since she'd been in the city, she'd come at the hardest times to walk in the park. She needed green around her, and Lucie had reminded her why. The world had looked different from up in that backyard apple tree.

The leaves were a softening frame. Everything was smaller. Everything was down there. She fantasized about stopping and hoisting herself up into a tree here, that really good one with the branches like arms just waiting to hold you and let you swing and dream and float, anything but fall. But she was too big now. And she was Ruby Maxwell. Climbing trees wasn't going to make the rest of the world get any smaller, any easier to look at. It wasn't going to diminish the remorse that had been her shadow since she was seventeen.

Back on the avenue, she crossed with the light. Even before she got to her building, she could see the reporter lurking outside it. She tucked her head and walked with determination. The doorman opened the door for her, just as the reporter recognized her. But he couldn't get past the doorman's stern look.

With any luck, she thought as she pushed the elevator's PH button, she could tell Paul why she hadn't come home last night, and then he could call his mother before she and his family arrived later this morning for the celebratory brunch. But when Ruby opened the penthouse door, Gracie was just taking off her coat and directing her staff toward the kitchen.

"Ruby!" Gracie said with surprise. "You're out and about early for you. It must be the excitement, can't sleep." Ruby could see Paul behind his mother. He didn't meet her eye.

Ruby smiled weakly at them.

"Don't mind me," Gracie rushed on. "I'm just getting Marcel settled in and helping with the crystal and all."

"I need a minute," Ruby said.

Gracie scanned Ruby's disheveled ensemble and waved her toward the bedroom. "Of course, of course, here you are the bride-to-be, and I'm holding you up. Go! Go!"

Ruby tried to catch Paul's eye, but he kept his away. "I'll need your help," she said to him finally. His face was absolutely ashen, and there was a slump in his shoulders she had never seen before. He was always so squared off, so upright and solid.

She went in and sat at her dressing table. It was the first morning in years that she had forgotten to put on makeup. She looked a ghost of the Ruby Maxwell who had taken Manhattan. But it was fitting. She felt as though she had slipped back into the ghost world that had been hidden inside her all along, the ghost world that played itself out in her dreams, haunted her. She looked like Ruby Blossom Bottom. She looked every bit that lost.

Paul came in finally and closed the door behind him. She exhaled and bit down on her lip to stave off the emotion. But already her hands were shaking, and she couldn't meet his eye. She had loved him all these years, loved him as her best hope and dearest friend. And she had needed him so much, needed the steadiness and the unquestioning acceptance. She had borrowed his certitude, used it as ballast in her ascent. There had always been Paul to hang on to. But she had to let go. She had to let go now.

"Paul," she managed at last. "I'm sorry. I owe you an explanation. . . ."

"Who have you been meeting at the Stanhope?" He bit off the words fiercely in a voice she hardly recognized as his.

She stood up, as though he had come at her and slapped her full across the face. Really, she would not have been more surprised if he had struck her.

He said, "You were there the night before last, as we both know. And your limo was there again last night."

"You followed me?"

His eyes glanced off hers. "Not personally," he said.

"You had me followed?"

"I hired someone . . . for your safety."

"For my safety?" She couldn't believe this. She couldn't. Not Paul.

"You have a high profile now," he said. "I was worried. You're my fiancée, remember? I have a right to worry."

"You have a right to worry, Paul, not to have me trailed without my even knowing it."

"If I had told you, you'd be self-conscious. I just wanted to have somebody watching over you in case anything came up. I wanted someone there to nip anything in the bud."

"Such as?"

"A stalker. There are crazies . . ."

He stopped when he saw the look on her face.

"You didn't trust me," she told him, but she was really

telling herself. *He didn't trust me.* Maybe she hadn't understood him any better than he had understood her.

He looked away from her, as though he could read her thoughts and they shamed him.

"How long?" she asked.

He hesitated. "Recently." She knew he felt how lame he was.

"Recently?" she prodded.

"You changed," he said heavily.

She sat back down at her dressing table.

He went on, justifying: "You said you'd marry me, but ever since then you've just stonewalled me. My mother is out there with her French chef, and my whole damn family is coming, and you won't let them announce it in the *Times*, you won't commit to a ring, you won't commit, period. You might as well have said no."

She swung her eyes up to his. "I should've said no, Paul. Because the truth is, I can't say yes."

He shook his head, turned up his palms as though he was asking her for something simple, something she could just place in his hands, turn over to him. If she only would. "What is it with you, Ruby? All these years, I've never asked anything of you, except that you'd be mine. And that's the one thing you won't give me. Then, finally, I think, finally, it's over, and you're going to make the commitment. But you suddenly become somebody I don't even know."

"I've always been somebody you don't even know," she told him. And there was real sadness in her tone. She was losing so much more than she had thought, in this moment. So much more.

He came over and knelt beside her, took her fingers in his. "No," he said gently. "You're wrong about that. I know all about you, Ruby Blossom Bottom."

It was as though his words had jerked a cord attached to her neck. Her eyes locked onto his. In all their years together, he had never said the name she had shed when she still believed she could somehow shrug off what hurt her so much to remember.

He let a sheepish smile slip out of one side of his mouth. "We've known the whole story from the beginning."

"We?" Ruby asked.

"My dad took care of it, right after you came to live with me. It was clear that whatever had happened to you in the past hadn't been easy. I didn't want to make you talk about it. You weren't offering. And they didn't think it was right, given everything . . ." He looked around at the opulence of the setting, of their home. "They didn't think they could just let some stranger into the house."

"Some stranger . . ." Her eyes left his face, went to her own in the mirror. And she seemed a stranger to herself in that reflection, a stranger with her daddy's blazing eyes and her daughter's pale skin and her mother's red, red hair.

He was waiting for her to go on. She stayed silent. Finally, he said, "It was nothing. Now that you're in the position you're in, you know that you can't be too careful."

Too careful. The words echoed in all the empty space inside her, all the vacuum of what she had felt for him and for his family, what she had trusted them with all these years.

"So, you know," she said icily.

"I know about your dad. . . . I know about the baby. . . ." His voice trailed off.

"Then why did you let me into your life?" She fixed him with her gaze.

"Because we all admired you for it," he said. "Coming from where you did and rising above it. It was an honest effort. I believe Dad said that your kind were the yeast that made this country rise to its present greatness."

The words rankled in her. *Her kind.* It seemed to her suddenly that she was no more than one of the silly social experiments he used to distract himself from renegade cells going haywire in the human pancreas. And worse, they admired her for the very thing that made her most despise herself.

"What does any of it matter now?" he said, stroking her fingers. "The point is I love you. I've always loved you, Ruby Maxwell or Ruby Blossom Bottom or Ruby Carrigan." He pressed his lips against the lines in the palm of her hand as though he could imprint himself there, loop their fates together, bind her to him. "I just don't want to lose you. I don't want to lose you to whomever it is you're meeting at the Stanhope. I don't want to lose you to your work. I just want what I've wanted since that first night I saw you at that party. I've wanted you to be mine. You, just as you are."

"I can't," she said. "I'm somebody else's wife."

The jolt of it ran through him. He lifted his face out of her palm, and the look in his eyes told her he hadn't known that. His father hadn't paid anyone enough to know that.

Chapter Nineteen

She was asleep, rising out of it as though from water that was too deep, as though her lungs might not hold. But she had to break the surface, wake up. She knew the arms were around her, felt bound by them to stay still and to be good and to take it. She felt the hands in her hair.

"Morning, Glory," her mother whispered.

Ruby sat up, broke free, filled her lungs. "Mama," she said. "You can't do this to me. You can't . . ." But she couldn't go on with words. It was too late. So many mornings, it had happened this way. Ruby had woken to someone stroking her hair, kissing her shoulder. And then they would have to lie there like that until her mama was calm and ready to let Ruby go, until Lila had absorbed enough of her daughter's spirit to go on herself. Sometimes Ruby made it to school just late enough to get a tardy. Sometimes she didn't make it to school at all. Down in town everyone thought it was her daddy who was Ruby's shackle, her daddy and the brothers who threatened to choke her out like weeds growing round a zinnia. But it was her mama she was always working to overcome. She got the grades, despite her mama. She took the job babysitting despite her mama, and later the job at the DQ. She learned to hear her own voice, despite her mama's voice inside her.

"What's the matter, Sis?" Lila said, sitting up, bewilderment all over her like hives.

"I'm not your doll, Mama."

"I know that. You're my baby girl, that's all."

"I'm a grown woman. You can't just climb into bed with me like that." She wanted to go on about boundaries and about what it had felt like to be six and twelve and sixteen and to have your mother holding on to you like that, like you were some baby doll who could keep away the shadows that lurked in the darkness. But she couldn't say it. She was too sad to say it. And anyway, it was too late for that.

Lila looked at her hands. "I've missed you," she said, as though she were speaking to her own fingers.

"I know, Mama," Ruby said, sitting back down on the bed. "I'm sorry for that."

"I'm sorry too," Lila said, looking over toward Ruby's eyes but then letting her own skitter away, scared or ashamed or accusing. Who really knew?

༱

 oad showed up with the morning papers, bagels, and a look on his face that seemed to try to make apologies for the whole world. Ruby was smeared on the front page of the *New York Post*. Worse, there was Lucie in her arms, startled as a deer in headlights. But it was the headline that most singed Ruby as she stared into the conflagration. RUBY MAXWELL'S SECRET SHAME CHILD? it inquired smugly.

Inside, with a six-page spread, there were pictures of Ruby's prosperous Fifth Avenue building juxtaposed with the blown-out facade of her parents' squat. There were also photos of her mother and her father, taken with long lenses in the unsuspecting days before Ruby went Rambo and rescued them, dragging them out to scrutiny and humiliation.

"I'm sorry, Ruby," Joad kept saying as he stood next to her, rolling himself backward and forward on the balls of his feet.

"Don't be," she said. "Nobody held a gun to my head and made me be famous." Although sometimes it had felt like someone had, someone inside her who was afraid to do anything else.

From what they could piece together (thanks to the fact that Joad played weekend football in Central Park with a sports writer at the *Post*), the paper had been working on a piece about the squatters already. It was just the kind of story that played well on the newsstand and might even nudge the paper into Pulitzer territory. For weeks, a couple of reporters had been pursuing it, trying to establish a rapport with the people who slunk in and out of the condemned buildings near Tompkins Square Park.

They had heard the rumors about people seeing Ruby Maxwell around trying not to look like Ruby Maxwell. But they had also heard the one about the space aliens who lived on the top floor of number 23 and the one about the fortune buried under the basement of number 46. Most of the squatters were tight-lipped and secretive, desperate to protect the illegal homes they had made in these tenements. It was the crazies and the kids who were eager to talk. Two urchins had bragged to the Pakistani newsstand guy who sold them Double Bubble that a lady from the television had given them $10 apiece, and the Pakistani newsstand guy had told the mob reporter who bought his Camel Wides there every morning and the mob reporter had told the squat reporter and the squat reporter had jotted it down in his notes. But it was Ruby herself who confirmed the rumors when she got out of a taxi and slammed into one Nick "The Knuckle" Dunsmore, who then told the squat reporter of the sighting and even pointed out the concealed door to watch, a door from which she did eventually emerge. Ruby imagined that just by stepping out that door she had made the reporter's night, if not his career.

"And one more thing, Ruby . . ." Joad said, leading her to the window and pointing down into the street. There they were: the press. She could see them on the steps of the Metropolitan, drinking steaming cups of coffee. She hadn't felt this way since the day she was nine and went into the brambles after blackberries. She'd come home covered with little seed ticks, and her mother made Wren and Simon hold her down while she tweezed the little parasites off Ruby one by one until they added up to 104 little bloodsucking pests. There weren't that many bloodsucking pests outside the Stanhope, but they made her every bit as miserable.

When they turned away from the window, they saw Lila, tears streaming down her face as she tore the newspaper into indecipherable bits that not even Lucie could puzzle back together, and in fact, later, when Lucie found the paper scraps, they must have looked like nothing more than confetti to her. Ruby caught her hanging out the bedroom window, letting the paper bits sift through her fingers and down into the avenue below.

Lila took her by the arm and led her away. Len bolted the window. But surely they had already taken her picture with a long, invasive lens. Ruby exchanged a look with her parents that said as much.

The secrecy was getting to them all. "I'm faunching to get outta here," Len groused.

Lila looked nervously at Ruby; they both knew that he was a powder keg waiting for the match. He wasn't used to being cooped up, especially cooped up without anything to "wet his gullet." He wasn't used to not having everything exactly according to his will. Ruby suspected he rued the day he had come out of that La-Z-Boy on his front porch and aimed his gun at Dewey, and also the night his house had burned, and also the day he had fled with the little girl to this city where anybody you said anything to might be the wrong person to say it to and it the wrong thing to say. They all rued those days.

CHAPTER TWENTY

*O*n Monday, the *RUBY!* show went off like the Ice Capades on thin, springtime ice. Everyone moved with an awesome grace, executing his or her job to the finest point and cueing the next person. The show glided along smoothly, looked sure and professional. There was the beauty in it of long practice paying off. It looked effortless. They skated their figure eights, landed their triple lutzes. But everyone was waiting, as she was, for the sound of the cracking ice, the splintering. Everyone was waiting for Ruby to fall through and be swallowed up by the cold depths.

She was aware of the spotlight, harsher now, and she abandoned herself to her performance—to the private one enacted only for the Muckety-Mucks and to the one before the cameras, where she read the papers and riffed on her own troubles like a blues player making music from pain. It was easy compared with going home to the

Stanhope and explaining to her parents (again) why they couldn't just go home to Kentucky right now while everything was stirred up and someone would be bound to follow them and hound, hound, hound. It was easy compared with the strain of not returning Paul's phone calls or Gracie's. It was easy compared with waking up in the dark of the morning and asking herself questions she couldn't answer, suspended as she was over some abyss gaping between her past and her future.

On Tuesday, it came to her on the way into the studio that she couldn't go on waiting with everyone else. She still had the power. She could still act, influence the outcome. First thing, she called Trev into the office and asked if he had the name of her mole. He hesitated and said that he did and that she wasn't going to like it. And she didn't, had known she wouldn't. It was Eden, of course. "Explain," Ruby said, and he told her how Eden had been going out with a guy whose roommate was in the mailroom at the *Post*. And they all thought it would do them some good. She'd blow off a little steam, something about a missed promotion, and the roommate would get a little notice, maybe his own promotion. All Ruby said to that was "Thank you." After he left, she sat and took deep breaths and when she had stoked up enough fire in her to care, she pushed the intercom button and said, "Cinderella, could you come in here?"

"You didn't promote me," Eden said in her defense.

"You didn't give me a chance," Ruby said.

"You said a year."

"Yes, I did. You're right about that. But sometimes, Eden, you have to let other people catch up to you. Life doesn't always fit into the time slots in your Filofax."

Eden glared at the edge of Ruby's desk. "I'm sorry," she said, although the words didn't resonate with any remorse.

"You will be, Edie. I'm afraid you will be."

And that was that.

Ruby had asked Joad to drive her along the Hudson that night, only because she wanted to keep moving, didn't want to be still with what was happening slow-motion. She had just gotten off the phone with the least favorite of the Muckety-Mucks, a guy who never wore socks with his Sundance moccasins and always wore jeans with a crease ironed down the front of each leg. He spoke with a British accent and couldn't keep his long fingers out of his hair. His voice stroked you the same way he stroked his hair, but she knew he was only soothing her along, waiting to see if the ratings were going to hold. She knew from Joad that her ratings had spiked but what he didn't say, because he knew she knew, was that the spike might just be the death watch. It might just be that morbid American propensity for watching somebody's final agony. Who could tell? She couldn't. She felt helpless, yet knew it was still within her power to help herself. It was just a subtle thing. It was about her own will, what strength welled up inside her.

And saving herself wasn't about saving the show. It

wasn't, she thought, as she watched the river running wide and slow beside the car. The only thing she knew for sure was that she had to keep moving. Walking had saved her when she was new to the city, back when the merest glance over her shoulder confronted her with the shadow of her own awful remorse. She had walked down Broadway, stopping for a bagel at H&H, and going on down and crossing the southern end of the park, turning back north when she hit Fifth Avenue. She had walked all the curving paths that lost themselves among the wild rock piles of Central Park and also those that wound under the trees clutching at one another in the far reaches. She had walked and walked and walked to find her own way past what she never could. And now that she couldn't so much as cross the street without an entourage of flashing strobes and grenade-tossed questions, Joad drove her and didn't tell her that they were being followed by at least three cars that he could see, although she of course knew that too. He played rap music and told her just to give herself to the beat, let it obliterate anything her head was trying to do to her. That night they went all the way up to Cold Spring, crossed the Bear Mountain Bridge, and came back down along the river on the Jersey side, came back to Manhattan and to the Stanhope and to the waiting for who-knew-what.

CHAPTER TWENTY-ONE

*T*he next morning, Ruby asked Joad to stop for the *Voice*, and even as she watched him go up to the newsstand and grin at the proprietor and start back toward the car with the newspaper in his hand, she knew somehow that this was what she had been dreading. This is what she had been waiting for.

Mack Lewis's cartoon was there. But however prescient she fancied herself to be, she could not have foreseen the cartoonist to be that merciless: There was her father, a drunken scrawl of a cartoon. He was sitting at a bar, while overhead on a television screen, the big-haired, spiky-heeled, wasp-waisted caricature of Ruby herself practically ate her microphone. The old man was saying how he had done Ruby wrong, how she had run away from home because of him. In the last frame, there was the child in Ruby's arms, coming out of the derelict building. The reader only had to add one plus one, no

compound fractions, no higher math required. The sum
was incest.

Ruby looked up from the paper and out the window
and into the face of her own billboard smile. It seemed to
say that she got what she had coming, that smile: You got
yourself slathered all over marquees, beamed up to satellite
dishes, and from there to the world, inflated into Macy-size
balloons. And then you got popped. She had been afraid of
it all along. She had ached for Oprah when the tabs kept
tabs on every inch of her waistline, every pound. She had
felt every blow dealt Hillary by those blowhards who called
themselves representatives. And maybe they were representative. Americans loved to see people struggle and pull
ahead, but there was something in them, some Puritan,
sniggardly streak, that rooted for the Conqueror to fall
short of the ultimate conquest: Barbra Streisand couldn't
get the Oscar as a director, nor Morgan Freeman as best
actor. Nancy Kerrigan should only get the silver, and then
she had to be seen as bad-mouthing Mickey so that everyone could bad-mouth her and say, "See, she was no princess. There are no princesses in America. We are all,
everyone of us, flawed. Not one of us is more than that.
Not one among us doesn't need the forgiveness of God."

Well, Ruby had never asked to be a princess. She had
only asked for a way to live with what she had done when
she was only a girl. She had only looked forward because
she could not bear to look back. If she had tried for success
every day of her life it would still have been only a fluke of

fate. She could not have manufactured it. She could not have set out to be RUBY! She had just worked everyday, opened any door that was set before her, climbed any staircase. And if all those days and doors and staircases added up to her becoming a celebrity talk show host, it had only happened to her the way other people's lives happened to them. She could just as easily have ended up a church organist in St. Paul or a heroin-hooked beach bum in Malibu. But fate had set her down in Shoulderblade, Kentucky, and taken her from there: from Dewey to the Bronx to Barnard to Paul to the congressman's campaign, then to the senator's, then the governor's, and onward to the network and to success and finally to this . . . this. . . . And now she had fallen from grace, been pushed by nothing more than a mistake. And it *was* a mistake, the kind of mistake the guy at the party had made about her, thinking her nothing more than Hollywood's Elly Mae. It was the kind of mistake that people made because they didn't have the suppleness of mind to allow for all the vast and wonderful possibilities for individuality in Appalachia and Harlem and Riverdale: People needed to keep one another in boxes with labels. They needed to simplify, reduce one another to something controllable. Otherwise, there was so much to fear.

"It's not true," she said aloud. Joad nodded his head like a guy in the front pew at church. He wasn't sure if she was talking to him or talking to God or talking to herself. It wasn't true, what the *Voice* implied. But then, it never was. Or rarely. And what if it were? Whose business was it but hers?

Ah, but there she couldn't acquit herself. Not really. Ah, there they had her. And maybe it was justice to be made to suffer publicly what she had suffered silently all this time that the show had been running: She had made people turn and look at their shadows. She had made them look at the darkness cast off by their living, their loving, their breathing. And now she was looking at her own, at the distortion of her own.

Hers was probably no more or no less distorted than what she got people to reveal on stage in the bright, harsh lights that threw longer, harder-edged shadows than the sun did. Mack Lewis had examined her life under unnatural light too, drawn his conclusions from that. Only she knew for sure how wrong he was, and for everyone else, it was entertainment. Her life, her warped *Village Voice*–generated life, was a circus. But it was her kind of circus. It was what had made her wealthy and famous. It was what had made her *RUBY!*

She just had to get through this show, she told herself as Joad swung into the lot. Just this one more time. Afterward, it was over. She wasn't going to do this anymore because she knew that there was no place far enough away from this where Joad could drive her.

I stumped my toe and down I go, she told herself bitterly. *Down I go.*

CHAPTER TWENTY-TWO

The press was an invading horde under the *RUBY!* awning. "Don't move," Joad told her when he pulled the car up. Obviously, the *Voice* had sent out its own press release, touting its scoop, trying to get the others to mention it as a spur to their own newsstand sales. Freedom of the press, she scoffed to herself. Freedom of the marketplace.

Joad picked up the phone and dialed inside for the the security guards. Three of them came out and wrapped themselves around Ruby and got her inside so quickly that the barrage of questions barely grazed her. Joad had a protective arm hooked around her waist.

Inside, the office was silent around her. She held on to Joad's arm, wouldn't let him leave. When they closed the door of her office suite behind them, she took both his hands in hers and said, "You can't leave me."

"I'm right here," he said.

"I want you with me all day. I want you working in here, not out in the car."

"Just today?"

"Just today," she said slowly. "This is going to be it."

"It?"

"Finis," she said.

"You're not a quitter," he scoffed.

"Watch me and see," she dared him.

"I'll stay," he said. "Just don't go freaky-deaky, that's all I ask. Don't quit."

"You'll stay." She took her phone list from the temp who had replaced Eden. (Joad pointed out that the girl looked like Olive Oyl, which at least made Ruby crack a smile.) After that, she called Trev in and told him he was fired. He stood right there in front of her desk with his mouth open for maybe two whole minutes. She found herself looking at one huge silver filling in a lower left molar, not believing what she was doing at least as much as he was not believing it. But it was her privilege to let him go. It was in her contract that she could hire and fire. She had gone along with him all this time only because she knew enough about the Muckety-Mucks to know that it was in her best interest to keep them well inside their comfort zone. Well, now everything was about her zone. And Trev belonged nowhere near it. She wanted this one last satisfaction of power.

When the door closed behind him, she looked at Joad. "You're Trev now," she said.

He held up his hands in disbelief and dismay. "I'm a limo driver."

"You're a Princeton summa cum laude. Now shut up."

They both laughed, and it was that laugh that got her into the rest of the day. She did the Green Room, just to steady herself. But she was deep inside herself in a silent, numb place from which she couldn't struggle free.

She didn't go into the soundstage until it was time for the cameras to roll. It was all she could do to snap off her opening monologue as the *RUBY!* intro music ebbed away. It was all she could do to keep the conversation lobbing back and forth as her guests talked about adoption snafus. She opened the floor to audience questions sooner rather than later.

That was her mistake.

"Ruby," said a man in the third row, "my question is for you. I'm from *Inside Edition*. We want to hear your answer to today's *Village Voice*. We want to know who this child is."

She stood stunned as the man unfurled a large picture of Lucie, waved it into the camera. The audience shifted its gaze from her to the standing man, from her to the man. It began to feel like the U.S. Open. His face came into focus, but she didn't recognize him as anybody she knew. Of course, they would have had to send a neophyte, someone security wouldn't recognize. Something surged up inside her, something old and ravening.

"Go to commercial!" the stage manager squawked because Trev wasn't there to do it and because Joad was still trying to figure out how to get the headset adjusted to his head. "Stop right there. Security!" The poor stage manager was flapping around in front of the audience.

"No," Ruby called. "Let's hear this, all of us." A gasp rose from the crowd. But she looked at Joad, and he nodded. His expression said, *Go, girl.*

Then, she fixed her gaze on the reporter, whose brow was lacquered in sweat. He blinked rapidly. "What do you want to know?" she asked him, point-blank. All breathing seemed to cease in the room.

He hesitated, seemed to marshal his tongue, then stammered, "Did you bear your father's child?"

Every muscle tightened, her fists clenched. Even expecting something of the sort, Ruby found that the question paralyzed her like the bite of some venomous spider. Outrage leached into Ruby's throat like bile, but though her mouth moved, it made not a sound. She felt the silence spread from inside her, out into the room. She tried again to put her lips around the answer. It didn't come.

Someone stood in the back row. "That child is my daughter," he said.

Ruby blinked into the lights, trying to see through them to the face. But she knew the voice.

A silhouette in the burning lights, he made his way down the aisle and up onto the stage. He stood between her and the audience, between her and the *Inside Edition* inquisitor in the third row. "Any questions you have about that child, you should ask of me," he said. His shoulders were set against the next blow, a fortress for her.

"Who are you?" someone called from the safe obscurity of an upper row.

"Dewey Maxwell."

Ruby stepped forward, stood shoulder to shoulder with him. She let herself look at him then and found that he was looking at her. He blurred through the tears in her eyes, but not before she saw what was in his. He gathered her to him, and she couldn't help herself anymore. She cried into his neck. The red light kept burning; the camera kept watching.

Chapter Twenty-Three

Ruby ran from Dewey's embrace into her dressing room, where she wept into her hands. It was too much. She'd dreamed him this real in the intervening years, dreamed that rough grain of his hands from working in his gardens, felt those hands on her face on her neck on her lips. But now he was here, and she was overwhelmed by the flesh and blood of him, by his scent of autumn smoke and his heat of sun-baked rocks and by the shell of his ear pressed cool against the flush of her cheek. All this time, she had leaned more toward his being dead: because otherwise, wouldn't he have found her?

Somebody knocked, then knocked again. Finally, Joad leaned into the room. "Yo," he said in the softest possible voice.

"Hey."

"Can I come in?"

"You're already in, Joady," she managed to point out.

He shrugged and closed the door behind him, stepped over to her. She shook her head, tried to shake off the gales coming over her, and only wept harder. These were the kinds of tears that pushed up unbidden, just throttled you, surprised you, made you know that there were things inside you that you had forgotten or never recognized, volcanic feelings that were building up, waiting for the moon to pull one way or the earth to shift. She tried to stop and couldn't. She had cried this way once when Paul had been making love to her, once when he had moved her in a way that had been only Dewey's, maybe. She didn't know then, couldn't know. But she had cried and tried to make herself laugh, which had only made her cry harder, and she had lain there naked in his arms, naked inside herself too and desolate, so full of some loss she couldn't have put Dewey's name on or Lucie's, because it belonged so much to her, belonged so deep inside her where no one could touch her but by chance, by some pull of the moon or shift in the earth.

Joad swept an arm around her suddenly, pulled her over to him. He was all bones, and she clung to him.

"He's waiting out there," Joad said when things seemed to be subsiding.

"Yeah?"

"Yeah."

She sat down hard in her makeup chair and looked at herself in the mirror. Her face was twisted out of shape and smeared with mascara and kohl liner. The sight made her cry harder at first and then laugh and then laugh harder until she was hanging on to Joad to keep from slumping to the floor.

"I need some help with my face," she said when words could squeeze past the hysteria.

Joad concurred. "Want me to get Fritz?"

She nodded. "And Joady?"

"Yeah?"

"Do you think you could be my driver again, for one last spin?"

He shot her his pistol finger, as in, *Of course.*

$\mathcal{J}$oad pushed some button up front that had never been touched, and a one-way window slid between the driver's side and hers. Then, he pulled the limo out of the studio lot, headed north. Ruby's cell phone was off, and the answering machine was taking care of the car phone. Olive Oyl was dealing with the Muckety-Mucks, who were sure to have something to say about the show going haywire. But Ruby couldn't think about that now, couldn't think anything, could only feel that she had escaped into her own dreams and that no one was going to wake her and cast her out: He was here.

Dewey sat deep in the leather seat facing hers. If she leaned her legs one way, they would touch his. But she didn't.

"You're not dead," she observed.

He smiled sheepishly. "Why do I think I'm going to wish I were?"

"You might as well have been," she said tartly, although it was all she could do to stay back in her seat, all she could do not to reach for him.

He sighed and shook his head. "Ruby, try to understand. I was the one who ruined your life."

"You didn't ruin my life, Dewey. You got me pregnant."

"Same thing."

"It didn't have to be."

"Tell your dad that."

She nodded, acknowledged the sober truth of what he said, and they sat there in a silence that confronted them with the memory of that desperate time, when circumstances had driven the wedge between them, forced them apart.

Dewey had cried when she told him she was pregnant. They were lying in his big iron bed, and the words hung over them like a thunderhead. "Are those happy tears or sad?" she had asked, completely stunned to reach over and find his face wet.

He hadn't been able to answer for the longest time. And then all he managed was "Forgive me, Ruby."

She had dredged up a laugh for him. But she didn't remember ever laughing much after that. She felt, in fact, that someone had knocked the wind out of her with one swift kick. She had felt the way she did when she was eight years old and fell out of the apple tree, flat on her back and empty, completely empty. It had hurt so much to try to get new air into her lungs that she'd thought she would rather die. She felt just that way when her mama seemed to know her secret by osmosis and said, "You better tell Dewey Maxwell to get himself out of town." Maybe it would've been better if he had gotten himself out of town, if they both had. But she had stayed and asked him to leave only until the baby came and then everything would be different, because she had been naive enough to believe that having a baby of her own would make her an equal to her parents. She had believed that when she had her own child she wouldn't be theirs anymore. She'd had to talk Dewey into it, sitting in his porch swing and going back and forth and back and forth as he moved from anger to resignation. He was only going because she wanted him to, he agreed finally, and only until the lilacs bloomed again.

Ruby had pushed herself through the pregnancy as she did through the birth itself, all of which had been a blur to her ever since, a blur of pain and confusion. But she had gotten through it not to see the baby but to see Dewey again. When she held her daughter, she searched the face for his face, and found him there in the infant's eyes but also found her mother's voracity and her father's fury and her own red hair. She named her Lucie Baltet, after Dewey's favorite copper-colored lilacs, and she waited for Dewey to come back up to Shoulderblade after them.

When Liza got the message to him and when Dewey

came for them, Len had been drinking. He was sitting on the porch in his old La-Z-Boy, shooting squirrels out of the oaks on the edge of the woods. He lowered the sights on Dewey.

"Get on out of here," Len had said, as Ruby had come out of the house with the baby, who was wailing to be fed.

"I've come to see my daughter," Dewey said, holding up his hands.

Len fired off a shot that kicked up a crater at Dewey's feet. Dewey stopped, looked to Ruby for help. She was scrutinizing her father, judging him. She had an odd, loud thought in her head that she would never forget afterward: *Why don't I have on real shoes?* That had stayed with her, that frustration at being hamstrung by cheap rubber flip-flops. Already, just looking at her dad, she had known that the moment was going to hinge on her own two feet, on her ability to run.

"Get on," Len barked.

"Ruby?" Dewey called. His voice seemed to hold out his arms to her.

"Daddy?" she pleaded. Len moved his gun up, centering it on Dewey, then he slid his eyes over to hers, making sure she knew what he meant. She saw the liquor brimming in them.

Dewey took another step toward her.

Ruby shifted her gaze to him. He had pushed more than he should've with Len that full of rotgut. He loved her. She put the baby up over her shoulder and stepped down off the porch. The bullet got to him before she did. She heard the air rip with it, heard the trajectory of her own shriek. She saw the blood.

"Stop, Ruby!" her father bellowed. "I'll aim six inches over this time, get him right through the heart."

But she was running now, outstripping her own good sense. Then suddenly everything splintered into snapshots and snatches of sound: She fell. Some mothering instinct in her made her lurch in midair so that she would land on her other shoulder, keep the baby from hitting the ground. She was aware of her elbows clawing at the dirt to right herself again and aware of the frustration at not being able to untangle her legs. She knew that her left shoe was gone.

Her father clicked back the trigger, and to her it sounded loud as a shot itself.

"Go on, Dewey," she cried. "Go on."

The baby must have gone on wailing, and her mother must still have been sobbing on the porch; there must have been sound. But Ruby remembered only the silence of the last look she and Dewey exchanged. It was such a mute, helpless, vanquished exchange. They were already lost to each other, though he still stood there in the driveway where later the chickens would pick around as though nothing had happened. She still lay there in the dust.

Later that night, Len Bottom had sat on the porch in a drunken pitch of feeling and had cried sloppily onto her neck, begged her to forgive him, begged her to forgive him the alcohol because that's what it was, that and loving her so much, his only little girl, loving her times two now that Lucie was there. "Forgive me," he'd asked. "Forgive me."

She hadn't. Not then. Not ever. She hated him for the fearsome hold he had on her, the fearsome hold times two. She had gotten up and walked down into town in nothing but her flip-flops. She had walked seven miles to the police. When she got there, she had muddy streaks on her face from crying, and you couldn't tell what color her clothes were. She looked made of dust, felt made of it. They'd tried to make her feel better as she charged her father, but they were country police and cousins besides. They never went looking for any injured party. They never put out a search for Dewey and his truck. They just drove her back home and took her dad away to "cool down" in the wire jail cell, where she was sure they all shared a bottle with him and played poker to make the nights pass. If Len had kicked up a fuss to go home, they would've let him.

She had called a number she had for Dewey's parents, and his mother had said they didn't know where he'd gone. And when she'd asked who was calling, Ruby had hung up, too afraid to admit who she was and what she had gotten the woman's son mixed up in, too ashamed.

$\mathcal{D}$ewey leaned forward in his seat. "You took my name," he said, breaking into her memories.

She smiled. "You gave it to me."

"I did?" He quirked an eyebrow, teasing her.

"Up on Rain Crow Mountain, remember?"

"Did you really think I could forget?" he asked her, suddenly solemn.

"I didn't see any evidence that you hadn't."

He bent closer. He was so close. "I couldn't forget, Ruby," he promised. And she knew just by looking into his purple eyes that he hadn't forgotten that autumn day before her parents had found out about the baby, when she and Dewey had walked up the mountain again and he had picked her a bouquet of Queen Anne's lace and goldenrod and chicory. The flowers had made her sneeze as she stood by the creek, which had slowed from its spring rush into a mossy gurgle, as she had stood there facing him and promised to be his wife and to take him as her husband. It wasn't binding under any authority but their own. But that had been enough for her, hadn't it? All these years, that had been enough.

"Ruby," he breathed.

And without knowing she was going to do it, she leaned toward him and reached for his temple. "You have white hair here," she said.

"One for every year we've been apart, that's all." He laughed.

She wrapped a strand of the white hair around her finger. And on impulse, she pulled.

"Ouch," he said, looking into her eyes. His breath was a breeze on her face.

She coiled another around her finger, pulled it too.

Then, another. His eyes never strayed from hers, though he flinched every time she yanked another hair from his temple.

"There," she said, when she had the last strand loose between her fingers. "All gone. Those years never happened."

He brushed his lips against hers. "Yes, they did," he said. "I counted every hour. Every minute. Every second."

"Me, too," she said.

He kissed her then, deeply enough to take them back in time, far back past the gunshots and the years apart that had turned him white at the temples, farther back to the nights of the blue moon when she had leaned against his chest and felt the vibrations of his poetry even as she heard the words drift away into the night, drift away with the scent of the new-mown grass. She heard again the crickets hiding in the rock foundation of the little cottage. She felt the dew coming on under her bare feet and saw the fireflies floating higher, flashing, floating higher as the hour grew later and the night pulled itself toward day and he pulled himself to her and she to him.

*J*oad buzzed from the front seat. She couldn't believe it. She'd told him to hold everything, not to let anyone or anything disturb this one hour of her life, please.

"Ruby?" he said over the intercom. "Uh, Ruby, I'm sorry. I know you said let the voice mail get the phone, but it's been ringing nonstop, and I had a feeling it was your office and so I picked it up 'cause I was just gonna tell Olive Oyl to hang tight, that you'd call her when you got a chance, but—"

"What?"

"You need to call your mother. Right now."

CHAPTER TWENTY-FOUR

*L*ucie was gone. They had caught her springing up and down on the sofa, watching Ruby on television. "Look, it's Sis!" she kept crowing. They hadn't seen any harm in letting her watch, and when they started to, they had been too astonished themselves to get the remote away from her. She had seen her own face on the newspaper. She had heard the awful question. She had witnessed Dewey's move down the aisle and onto the stage with Ruby. Lucie knew everything.

Lila had blamed Len, and Len had blamed the whole goddamn world, and when they looked around, Lucie was gone. She wasn't in the bathroom, nor her bedroom, nor theirs. She had slipped out of the suite.

Joad was trying to get Ruby and Dewey back into the city, but everybody from Westchester seemed to be competing with them for the four lanes and the narrow bridges. The sun was going down in a polluted swirl of color over New Jersey, and the Hudson looked as though it had been set ablaze. The world seemed to be burning, Ruby along with it. Dewey held her hand, but his face had gone white and tight. Neither of them spoke. He had never seen his daughter's face, except on the leering front page of a newspaper. He had never even seen her, and now this.

When they were headed down Fifth, Ruby leaned into the window toward Joad. "Go to the Stanhope first. I'll get out and let them all see me. Then I'll come right back out and get in the car, and you'll go to the apartment, drop me off. I'll go in the front door. You'll pull away. They'll stake themselves out. You'll go around three blocks and circle back to the service entrance. I'll be waiting for you."

He braked at the Stanhope. Dewey waited as she ran the gauntlet of reporters. The doorman kept the surge back as she emerged into the lobby. The Man in Charge rushed to greet her. "We're doing everything we can, Ms. Maxwell. We're searching every linen closet, the boiler room."

"Give my parents a message," she told him. "Tell them I'll be back in fifteen minutes. And tell those bloodsuckers outside that we've checked out." Then she wheeled and left.

Back through the reporters she went. Their flashes sparked. Their questions swiped at her. But they were a comfort in one way, their slashing questions: They weren't about Lucie missing. They didn't know she was gone. Bless the Man in Charge for that, at least.

Joad eased away from the curb. "Go slow," she told him.

He led a parade of reporters the few blocks to her apartment building. She hoped she wouldn't run into Paul, whose calls she still had not returned. But she had to take the chance. When she emerged from the car, she looked around for a reporter from the *Times* whom she recognized. "Hey, Lutz," she said. "You're getting the exclusive. To-morrow."

"C'mon, Ruby," the others protested. Joad pulled away from the curb.

She made her way through the crush to the doorman on duty. He was holding the door open with one arm and holding back the reporters with his other. "Welcome home, Ms. Maxwell," he said.

"Keep 'em busy," she told him through a slit of lips. He looked at her a second, got her meaning, then stormed out into their midst, crying foul.

Ruby went through the building, out the back entrance, where all the deliveries were made, and got into the limo. Dewey was shaking his head.

She shrugged. "Like a rat through a maze," she said.

Not a single journalist was at the Stanhope, certainly not near her side entrance. She and Dewey slipped in un-noticed. Joad took the car to double-park outside the pent-house, reenforcing the notion that she was there.

Lila's face rushed to Ruby's when she opened the door, then fell in disappointment. Len came charging out of the bedroom. "It's only you," he said. Then Dewey stepped into the room, closed the door.

Len's arms raised in the air as if pulled by some unseen puppeteer. He hissed, "You're the whole goddamn reason she's gone."

Ruby stepped between them. "He's her father," she said.

"I'm the only father she knows," Len said, looking at her with withering defiance.

"We thank you for that," Dewey said. He took a few steps in from the doorway.

"You can't take her away," Len charged. But there was a quaver in it that, standing as close as she was, Ruby heard.

"Nobody can take her away," Ruby said, putting her hand on her father's chest. "She's run away."

"We have to find her," Dewey said calmly. "That's what matters."

Len turned and began to pace the room. "Could you stop that?" Lila said from the window. "You're gonna wear holes in that carpet."

"Shut up," Len snarled. And Ruby was glad that she'd kept him away from the liquor. He wasn't as nasty as he could be.

Dewey said, "Where have they looked?"

"Everywhere," Lila said. "They've looked the whole building over from cellar to attic. She's not here."

"She has to be," Ruby said, crossing to stand by her mother at the window.

A knock sounded at the door. Dewey went to investigate. He opened to the Man in Charge, who quietly explained that his people had been over the building, scoured it. He hesitated, cleared his voice. "Should I call the police?"

Ruby turned back to the window, as though she couldn't bear to look at what his words meant. She watched people in evening clothes climbing the steps into the Met and realized that she and her Vera Wang and her Maud Frizons were missing the benefit. All that belonged to somebody else, somebody who was already gone.

The Man in Charge shifted his weight behind her, and Dewey said softly, "Ruby?"

She didn't look away from the window. Lucie couldn't have gone out into the city, she told herself. How could she have slipped past all those reporters? And where would she have gone anyway? Ruby concentrated on the tourists sitting on the steps of the museum in the yellow floodlights that made the granite steps look blue. She looked at the children running up and down the steps and dangling their hands in the fountain. And suddenly, she was flooded through with hope.

CHAPTER TWENTY-FIVE

*R*uby went alone. She could trust Dewey to soothe Lila. And Len might as well get accustomed to the fact that Dewey was part of his life. It wouldn't hurt for them to recognize how much this child meant to each of them. And she wanted to do this. She needed to do this.

If there were reporters lurking, they didn't spot her. She crossed the avenue and made for the park, which was full of coming dusk and the early green light of the gas lamps. Ruby followed the cobbled path. She knew where she was going, what would draw her daughter as it had drawn her: the tree with the waiting arms, waiting to scoop you up and hold you up high, where everything down there looked small.

Under the tree, the ground was worn to polished dirt, no grass grew. This was a favorite spot for all the children in neighboring blocks who weren't growing up with apple trees in their backyards.

Ruby stepped onto the lowest branch, holding her breath before looking up, praying Lucie would be there, praying she would be there and safe.

Ruby lifted her eyes. And there, dangling just above her were the fast tennis shoes, their white bottoms glowing in the dusk.

"Lucie?"

"Yeah."

"You okay?"

"Yeah."

"It's getting dark. Aren't you scared?"

"Look," said the child, "I can hang upside down." And she did. Her braids, hanging down, practically brushed Ruby's head.

"Beautiful, Goose, really." She watched Lucie a minute, then said, "Would you like to go home?"

The child was singing to herself, paying Ruby no mind: "*Oh my darling, oh my darling, oh my darling Clementine . . .*"

Ruby climbed up onto a higher branch, hooked her legs around it, let herself fall backward, dangle. She looked at Lucie, eye to eye, upside down.

"To Shoulderblade?" Lucie asked.

"Is that where you wanna go?"

"Yeah."

"To Shoulderblade then," Ruby answered. "I'm sorry about everything, Lucie. We didn't mean to hurt you."

Lucie sang some more to herself with her eyes closed. "*You are lost and gone forever, oh my darling Clementine . . .*"

"It just means there are more people who love you," Ruby said.

Lucie opened her eyes. "Am I still supposed to call you Sis?"

Ruby's eyes burned. "You can call me anything you want. As long as you call me something."

"Okay, Something," Lucie said, reaching over for Ruby's hand. Ruby reached back. They curled their fingers together. They pulled each other back and forth, singing another verse of "Clementine" very softly.

"What about him?" Lucie asked when Ruby was beginning to feel the blood throbbing in her ears. "What am I supposed to call him?"

"You don't have to think about this now," Ruby said. "You can get used to everything. Then later, when you feel like you're ready to meet him, you can call him whatever."

"Oh, great." Lucie sighed, rolling her eyes. "Something and Whatever."

And they stayed that way a while longer, upside down with the blood pounding in their ears and Ruby wondering how she was going to get down without killing herself. But they stayed, swinging while the rest of the world was down there and small enough to suit them.

CHAPTER TWENTY-SIX

*I*n the elevator down the next morning, Ruby told herself that she knew all about walking away from something. She told herself that walking away from *RUBY!* was not going to be anywhere near as wrenching as rising in the gray before dawn and touching those little curled fingers one last time and turning and going. It was not going to be that hard. Because it was not going to be wrong and weak and cowardly.

She had thought so often of that leave-taking these last days, examined the memory, turned it over in her hands like the skeleton of a bird whose death was a mystery to her. She understood that she had been already gone, inside. After the cops had taken her dad into town, she had sat limply on the stump where the sweet william grew. Wren was sitting in the grass beside her. "You're like a scarecrow lady," he said, touching her knee. "Nothing but straw and empty eyes, somebody else's old clothes." And she had told him she didn't know how she could live with things as they were—without Dewey and with this little baby girl and without any prospect of making life any better, ever. "I was the crow before," she said. "I was the bird."

"I know."

"Being with Dewey was like having wings."

"That wasn't Dewey," Wren said. "You've always had wings."

She shook her head.

He said, "Fly."

One thing she had known: She couldn't be at Shoulder-blade when her dad came home from jail. She couldn't look at him. Wren and Liza had helped her devise the way for her to leave with the baby. But the night before she was to meet her cousin at the bus depot, she had found Lila sitting in the swing, singing to the baby. She looked up at Ruby and said, "I'd die without this little bit of sunshine." And so when Ruby had risen before the next dawn, she couldn't bring herself to take her little daughter. Something in her clamored that she didn't know how to fend for herself, much less this vulnerable child. Something in her couldn't bear to leave her own mother with nothing at all. And so she had left Lucie in the cardboard box that was her cradle.

Ruby had told herself that she would come back for Lucie when she could do right by her, when she had the necessary things to give her. But somehow, she never felt she had them. She had money, after a while, and she sent a great deal of it. She had a home. But, inside, she was barren. There was nothing inside her that would do a child any good, and any way, she could never get past that great barrier of shame that lay between her and Shoulderblade. Once she was gone, it became impossible to imagine herself crossing over into that terrible realization of what she had done. She could never imagine herself going home.

Even though the reporters were back, Joad was shooting imaginary baskets as she approached the car. "Hear that?" he asked.

"What?"

"*Swish*," he said. "*Swish, swish, swish*."

The cameras were clicking. Ruby was ignoring questions.

She tweaked her mouth at him as she climbed into the car. He winked. Dear old Joady, she was going to miss him. He'd stayed last night to make sure Lucie was safe, and then he'd even taken Dewey down to his hotel in Times Square. Dewey hadn't wanted to meet Lucie when she was traumatized. He had wanted to wait. And Ruby couldn't blame him, thought it was right. Everything now was so tainted by this fame hoopla. She had leaned against Dewey last night, saying good-bye and apologizing for that, and he had quoted Emily Dickinson: " 'Fame is a bee,' " he said. " 'It has a song, It has a sting. Ah, too, it has a wing . . . ' "

"Let's hope," she had told him, kissing him lightly on the lips. "Let's hope."

Joad *swished* again as he climbed behind the wheel. He handed back her Starbucks, also his copy of *Variety*. "Look at that," he said.

The headline stunned her: RUBY STAGES COUP. The story was a tight little piece about how, once again, Ruby Maxwell had turned a scandal into gold. With the governor and Plato's Retreat it had translated into a political victory. With Ruby herself, into a ratings-grabbing masterpiece.

"What?" she said aloud, in utter disbelief.

Joad chuckled gleefully in the front.

"They think I planned that?"

"You didn't?" He arched and twanged one eyebrow at her in the rearview mirror.

She twanged one right back.

*O*live Oyl appeared over her desk the minute she sat down. "Bone is here," she said.

Ruby had figured he would be. She nodded that she would see him and took a last sip of her Starbucks. She wished that Olive Oyl had Eden's habit of a morning bagel but, then, she was glad the temp didn't have some of Eden's other habits. Ruby dug around and settled on eating an old peppermint Lifesaver she found in her top desk drawer.

"Bone," she said, with a fondness that was almost nostalgic now that her days as *RUBY!* were nearly over.

Bone himself bent to kiss her. He was all grin.

"Try to look a little sorry," she said.

He said, "I was up until three brainstorming with the team about what positions to take on this new contract negotiation—"

"Whoa, there's a huge assumption," Ruby interjected.

"My phone rang at six this morning," he said. "Jonah Conrad from network contracts. He was on the point end of the spear. His phone had been ringing from both coasts all night long."

"And the gist?"

"The gist is you're as golden as the Emmy statue, Ruby. You are a capital *Q* when it comes to the *Q* ratings. They want you at all cost."

She shook her head. "Do they really think I engineered that yesterday?"

Bone chortled, giddy with power. "They don't care. That was television nirvana, made-to-order by the broadcasting gods."

"That was my life," she said quietly.

Bone tried to tone down his glee, but it still seeped through. "Your life is worth a lot to them, then," Bone said. "What do you want? Anything. The big blue is the limit."

"Out," she said. "I want out."

"No, you don't," he scoffed.

"Yes."

"No, you don't. You can name your price."

"I have a daughter, Bone. I'm sure you've read the papers."

"Lots of women have kids and careers. Look at Demi Moore," he said. "Look at Katie Couric and Kathie Lee. Hell, look at Rosie. She does it all alone. Here, call her. Let her talk some sense into you." He whipped his micro cell phone out of his breast pocket.

She shook her head. "I want to teach my daughter how to suck the nectar out of roadside honeysuckle . . ."

He snorted.

". . . and how to make ice cream out of the second snow of the year and how to catch fireflies . . ."

"Ruby, you're being ridiculous. I'm not going to let you do anything hasty, not while all your hormonal instincts are firing like this all of a sudden. I'm not going to let you harm yourself. I'm not."

She shrugged "I want to go home."

"You are possibly the most powerful woman in television, right on Oprah's tail, anyway, and you can define yourself. You can live your life any way you want to. And you are not going to tell me that you don't want what you've worked this hard for. You're just not going to tell me that. I saw you in the Bronx, Ruby, remember? I've seen you work until three A.M. I've seen you eating Maalox like M&Ms. I've seen you before they put the makeup over those rings under your eyes. I know what this has cost you." He struck the desk methodically with the flat of his hand.

She looked down at her own hands. She knew he knew. And she knew too.

"What good are you going to be doing your daughter by quitting?" Bone said. "You want her to think that women live by honeysuckle and babies alone? It doesn't have to be one or the other. Think about it."

She did.

"Can I be Barbara Walters?" she asked finally.

A grin spread across his face like the sun coming out from behind clouds. "Ruby, you can be anyone you want to be."

"And Joad?" she asked. "Can he be anything I want him to be?"

Bone studied her a minute. "Yeah," he said. "Sure."

Ruby smiled. "Okay," she said. "Joad is Trev now."

Bone looked at her another long minute. "Joad is executive producer," he said, as he made the note on his Newton. "Okay, next."

"I do a single prime-time show for every season, an in-depth kind of thing, where I sit down with someone who has a story to tell and needs someone who will let them tell it their way—with just a wee bit of coaxing, you know, my way."

"Your way . . ." Bone said as he made the note.

"My way."

CHAPTER TWENTY-SEVEN

The penthouse was polished with sunlight. Ruby stood amid the last of her boxes, raised her face to the arched windows, and listened to the quiet life of the rooms, which would go on without her. She had found a new place overlooking the park from the West Side, where the neighborhood was livelier (and more colorful, as Joad liked to point out) and where there was a playground just inside the park and where they could walk to see the dinosaurs in the Natural History Museum on any little whim. She hoped it would come to that. Anyway, Joad would be close. They could walk to Barney Greengrass for breakfast on Sundays. If the Baldwins could do it, she could too.

She turned and went back into her dressing room. The clothes and shoes had been packed specially, color coded, and taken to the new address and unpacked there yesterday. The dressing room was empty. She crossed to the bed, touched the tapestry spread she had been so thrilled to find and, as she did, the movement caught her eye in the mirror. There she was: still Ruby Maxwell. And yet not. In the space of time it had taken Fritz's eyeglass collection to go from 206 to 208, everything for her had changed.

The front door closed. She hoped he had come alone. "Ruby," he called.

"In here," she said.

Paul filled the doorway. She hadn't seen him since the day of the brunch that was never going to be. They had taken care of everything by phone. "Are you sure you want to do this?" he had asked.

"I'm sure," she had answered.

"Because I'm not, Ruby. I have to tell you."

Something had tugged at her when he had said it, some old longing for everything he could give her. Not the Fifth Avenue address, nor the Danish bed. Not his name. Not all the whispered temptations in Bryan Ferry. Just to be in Paul's calm aura, his place in the world, the one that moved with him and made him feel at home wherever he was, never lost.

But *her* place surrounded her now, moved with her. She had to remember, get used to believing it.

She looked around the sunlit apartment. The rooms still looked very much the same. Her absence would hardly dent the place. She had insisted on leaving all the antiques, all the pieces they had found on their forays together. They belonged to his world, not hers. Anyway, she needed to start all over, buy only painted primitives maybe or waxed and golden furniture from old French farmhouses, things with nicks and chips and caved-in places, things that revealed everyday living in their scars.

"Everything's packed," she told him. "My books, mostly, some music."

He held up his hands as though he trusted her and couldn't bear the litany.

"You're going to be better off, Paul," she said. "Really, you are."

He smiled wanly, moved to the window. "Sure I am."

"I do love you." She couldn't help telling him.

He shrugged. "But not that way."

"Which way is that?"

"The only way that matters."

She went to stand by him. She knew someone would love him the way it mattered and told him so. It would just be a question of time passing and him letting it happen. He already had tickets to sail the Galápagos; Gracie had made sure and told her—as proof that her son would go on without Ruby, be just fine, better, even. Sailing the Galápagos was a start.

He reached for her hand. And they stood together looking out the window and down on the part of the world that came and went along Fifth Avenue. Everything down there looked so small and simple from up here, from up here in their treehouse.

"Okay," she said, drawing in a breath.

"Okay," he said.

She kissed him on the cheek, and before she left, she saw him reach to touch the lipstick souvenir.

CHAPTER TWENTY-EIGHT

*J*oad held the door open for her at the airport. He had insisted on taking her. "One last airport run," he'd told her, even though he already had the new driver trained in how to blinker and nudge the car into traffic and how to manipulate the CD changer and how to order Ruby's Starbucks. Joad had taken her parents and Lucie to LaGuardia weeks before, Dewey even before that. They had all decided that it was best to take Lucie back to the mountains, let her get used to the idea of who Dewey was to her, who Ruby was to her before she had to get used to the reality of them. Lucie had kissed Ruby good-bye without letting go of Lila's hand.

Now, Joad foisted Ruby's luggage onto his shoulder and led her through the sliding doors. He walked her all the way back to the security gate.

"This isn't in the job description of an executive producer on prime time," she joked.

"Nope," he said. "It's in the job description of homie."

Tears seeped into her eyes, though she blinked hard.

"Dag, none of that."

She hugged him hard. And he had trouble letting her go. Even though they both knew they'd be on the phone six times a day between now and when she arrived back in a month to put in her face time with the Muckety-Mucks, gearing up. Until then, he was running the show. She'd told him to think of it as his. She was just the upfront talent. That's how she wanted it this time. She had a life to live, a lot of catching up to do.

CHAPTER TWENTY-NINE

*D*riving into the mountains from the airport in Lexington, Ruby felt as though she were still flying. She felt that her shadow passed over the plunging hollows and the peaked green hills like one thrown from a cloud moving on the high breeze. She did not remember the past, nor consider the future. Everything seemed utterly obscured by just this moment, the angle of the light falling on the roadside chicory, the insects whirring in the grass.

She was going home to the cottage. Dewey had bought it for nothing but back taxes. It was falling down around him, he had told her on the phone when she was still negotiating with Bone and unveiling Joad to the staff and doing her final daytime shows. She had been alarmed at that description, "falling down"—only Dewey laughed it off. He planned on shoring up the foundation and sistering some of the beams and sanding away the old paint on the clapboards and brushing on new, white with yellow shutters, he thought. "The lilacs are still blooming," he told her. "It's a sign." And she told him she was darn lucky he lived by signs, and he agreed.

It was a joke between them now because he'd told her how he'd taken the gunshot wound to his arm as a sign that he should just stay away from a sore situation that his presence could only make worse—for Ruby; the damage was done. He would just keep sending a check every month, so at least the little girl would know he cared. And then he had read Ruby's picture on *TV Guide* as a sign that by staying away he had done the right thing, hadn't ruined her after all. But then, he had come home to a fax from New York, a fax from the latest girlfriend he had refused to marry. She had moved to the other coast to get away from him, away from his memory of that woman named Ruby who was now showing up in every magazine just as she had always shown up in his dreams and his conversations and his excuses for why he couldn't commit. And there she was all over everything in New York: *RUBY!* It was supposed to be a joke when his ex faxed him the cover of the *New York Post* with a jot at the top that said, "How's this for a sign?" But to him, it really was a sign, a sign that he had wasted too many years not seeing that little girl's face, not knowing what Ruby felt. And that's when he had walked out on his teaching job and bought a full-price ticket to New York, which he couldn't afford after years of teaching public school in East L.A., and he had gone to the set of *RUBY!* Just in time.

Without that last sign, that fax, he might never have known that it was still possible to have Ruby's hand in his, to drive up Shoulderblade and meet a little girl whose face he had tried so often to imagine in the years since he had retreated down the mountain with blood pooling on the seat and found a doctor who would help without reporting the crime, in the years since he had gone west, ending up in Santa Monica because he'd exhausted the road, hit the ocean. He'd stood in the surf for a long time, that first evening, watching the sun get swallowed up by the Pacific, thinking how it was the way his hopes had been swallowed up by circumstance. "I blamed the stars," he had told her. "Who else was I going to blame?" And so, out of kinship or out of inertia, he had stayed in Los Angeles. He'd taught school in the poorest neighborhoods, lived with a series of women. And he might have gone on doing it, might have helped the kids the little he could, might have gone on trying to love the woman who loved him at the moment. He might have gone on being numb. Ruby might have too.

*H*e was waiting for her in the porch swing, the late-day sun limning him in a haze of gold. He got up and walked down the granite steps to the front walkway and then down the stone steps to the curb as she parked the rental. She got out and though some part of her still balked at the neighbors seeing, she went into his arms and was wrapped in his old affection, as comfortable to her as worn denim. He smelled of his garden, of the sun in his hair and the wind on his bare arms. They went to the porch swing and sat there, touching from shoulder to hip to ankle. She held his pinky finger in her hand.

"Tell me a poem," she whispered after the longest time when his one foot on the painted porch boards had kept them swinging steady as the pendulum on a clock, ticking away time that was theirs at last. "Something pretty."

" 'From you have I been absent in the spring . . . ' " he began. She closed her eyes and listened as he said each line until he got to the sonnet's end: " 'Yet seemed it winter still, and, you away, As with your shadow I with these did play.' "

She leaned to kiss him. "Thank you," she said into his lips.

Some time later, she told him, "I need to go see the lilacs." But still, they didn't stir. Out back, she knew, the last of the lilacs were blooming. They weren't as beautiful as they had been, as they would be again, he'd told her. All they needed was a thorough pruning come the end of the month, though, and a good dose of lime in the fall. All they needed was some time with him, he had bragged during that phone call. "Me too," she had told him. "I need some time with you."

"I'm waiting," he had answered.

The days had grown long, moving toward the summer solstice, but even so, the night was coming. Dusk seemed to rise up from the mown grass with the fireflies, to seep into the air like the scent of the honeysuckle twining crazily on the picket fence. The darkness seemed to belong to another moment. It seemed to belong to them the way the old darkness had when she had lain under the stars with her head in his lap, and he had spoken poetry to her that seemed to come from some place in him but also to echo from some place in herself, some place she had never before suspected. All these years since, she had lived alone in that deep place his voice had sounded out in her. Until now, until he had come back.

When the first whippoorwill called in the woods up the hill, he laced his fingers up in hers and led her across the porch. The screen door squeaked, and the wide pine floorboards creaked under their step. She saw the shapes in the rooms—a rocker, a floor lamp, the white face of a clock. She saw the curtains stirring like spirits at the window.

And then she did not see anything but the colors in the darkness that he had always conjured for her. She did not feel anything but his lips on hers, his lips on her shoulder, in the hollow between her breasts. He laid her down. She did not taste anything nor smell anything that wasn't him. He rose above her, covered her with his warmth. She did not hear anything but that old music of theirs, not the jazz on the record player, not the crickets in the old foundation, not that whippoorwill up the hill in the woods. They were together again in a darkness that belonged to them at last, and the only music was theirs.

CHAPTER THIRTY

The next morning, they were quieter than usual, even as Dewey cut flowers from the garden and mixed up a batch of cookies, even as Ruby made the bed and stuck her fortune on the refrigerator with a magnet: "Love does no wrong that can't be made right." Dewey kissed her when he saw it, and chuckled.

Later, her family would come for a picnic supper. But first, she and Dewey were going up to Shoulderblade for the house raising. She had arranged it long distance, spoken to each of her brothers. She asked their forgiveness in her way, and they gave it in theirs: They agreed to help rebuild a place for their parents. Ruby could've hired it done, as she had hired the architect and ordered in the materials. But she thought the symbolism was important. She thought they all needed to make this home, rebuild it from the ground up.

As they headed for the door to leave for Shoulderblade, Dewey caught her to him and kissed her deeply. Then he touched her forehead with his lips and said, "I'm a little scared."

"He's not going to shoot you this time," she teased. "I'm paying for his house, remember?"

"Not of him," Dewey said. "Of her."

"She's a little girl with strawberry-blond braids and Band-Aids on her knees. She won't hurt you unless you refer to her freckles as anything but sun kisses. Not freckles."

"Not freckles," he repeated, as though memorizing his role. Then he added solemnly, "Maybe it's just that I'm afraid of how much it's going to hurt every time I look at her, because then I'll be faced with all the days I couldn't, all the days that slipped away without my seeing her change from one to four to eight."

"I know," Ruby told him. "I know."

"Do you think she'll ever forgive us?"

"I forgave them," Ruby said, realizing that she had even as she said it. "Somewhere in there I learned to look at the world through their window, see things the way they do. She'll just have to learn to look through our window, see why we did the things we did."

He kissed her above the left eyebrow.

"Forgive yourself, Dewey. That's all we can do."

$\mathcal{U}$p the mountain, her brothers didn't come down off their ladders or off the roof, where they were laying shingles. She walked around the framed-in house, holding Dewey's hand, and each of her brothers looked down at her, smiled at her, bashful still. "Hey, Sis," they said. Wren hugged her, though, and kissed her on the ear because he missed her cheek in his embarrassment. He had tears in his eyes.

"Thank you," she told him, "for watching out for her."

He shrugged, then laughed. "She's got one hell of a savings account for a little squirt."

"I knew you wouldn't let him drink it," she said.

"Hell, no," he said gruffly, then grabbed her in a hug. "I didn't mean for you to fly the coop forever," he whispered into her hair.

"I didn't," she told him. "I didn't." She was standing-there proof.

$\mathcal{L}$ila was upstairs, and she leaned out a window hole and called down, excited as a child. "Come see, come see." Ruby climbed up a ladder where the porch would someday be. Her dad reached down and gave her a hand up into the skeleton house. When Dewey appeared after her, Len leveled his finger like a gun, then laughed an awkward, sheepish laugh. Dewey laughed that way too.

Len and Lila showed them this bedroom and that. Her

dad talked about the fireplace insert, and her mama showed Ruby where the kitchen was going to be.

"Paint it yellow, Mama," Ruby said.

"You better believe it," Lila said.

And they both smiled out the window.

$\mathcal{L}$ucie was up the apple tree.

Ruby went over to stand below it. Dewey followed a few steps back.

"Hey there, Goose," Ruby said.

"Hey there," Dewey seconded. Ruby heard the emotion riven through the marble tones of his voice. He was trying not to stare at the child, but he wasn't strong enough to fight the desire to see what he had deprived himself of all this time.

The little girl didn't look full at Ruby, and she couldn't even touch her gaze on Dewey.

Ruby said, "Lucie, this is who's been waiting to meet you. This is Dewey."

"Hi," he said, holding up his hand to shake.

Lucie hooked her knees around a branch, threw herself backward, and when she stopped swinging, she took Dewey's hand, shook it. She said, "Nice to meet you, Whatever."

CHAPTER THIRTY-ONE

*W*hen the shadows were long across the grass, Ruby's brothers came down to the cottage with their families. Raphy dutch-rubbed Ruby's head, and the rest of them slugged her in the arm. Their wives, most of whom Ruby had known on the playground growing up, brought potluck picnic dishes—deviled eggs and fried chicken and sour cherry pies—and their children brought chaos that climbed into the old fruit trees and rattled up the front stairs and down the back and that crowed and whined and giggled from every corner of the yard.

Liza came with her three little ones and their daddy, who had taken her back when she came home from the city. She was heavier than she had been, and her hair was frazzled on the ends from too many perms, but the children held onto her fingers and called her Mama. And she beamed down into their faces and called them honeybunch and sugar. Ruby looked at her and saw what might have been hers, two roads diverged in a wood. They hugged and cried and sat on the porch swing together. "You look happy," Liza told her. And Ruby threw back her head and laughed. "I am now," she said. "I am right this minute."

And then one of Liza's kids scraped a shin, and she said, "Oh, crud," and went to see what was available in the medicine cabinet, and anyway it was time Ruby got back in there and helped Dewey. Two redheaded nephews knocked heads under her feet as she came into the kitchen. "Now, I'm home," Ruby joked to Dewey, and he just smiled and went back outside with another pitcher of lemonade and a crock of tea.

In the yard, the kids had barely finished eating before they were getting up a game of The Needle's Eye. "We need more," they chanted in unison. "More." They tugged at their parents' hands, but everyone was languorous with food, comfortable sprawling on their blankets or leaning into the picnic table.

Lucie grabbed Dewey's hand. "C'mon, Whatever."

Ruby could see the pleasure come into his eyes. But he hung back, said, "I don't know how."

Lucie rolled her eyes. "It's easy." Then she explained elaborately with the help of her fluttering hands: "See, we all dance in a circle under the arch that those two are gonna make with their arms. . . ." She pointed to two of her big boy cousins. "And then we all sing and when they bring their arms down on you, you have to pick whether you want to be a hamburger or a hot dog. And then the hamburgers have to go against the hot dogs in tug-of-war, to see who can pull the other guys over. See?"

"I've forgotten how it goes, that song," he said, looking at Ruby. And she knew he hadn't.

"You'll remember," Ruby said, getting up and pulling him up after her. Lucie got between them, holding hands in the circle, and around they went, singing:

> *"The needle's eye that does supply,*
> *The thread that runs so true,*
> *Many a beau have I let go,*
> *Because I wanted you."*

Their daughter's voice rose up between them, holding them together as surely as did her clasping hands:

> *"Many a dark and stormy night,*
> *When I went home with you,*
> *I stumped my toe and down I go,*
> *Because I wanted you."*

Dewey's eyes glistened as he looked at Ruby over Lucie's head. The words echoed all through Ruby, through her memory of that first night in the porch swing and through the years that had separated them. The words were like a stone cast into still waters all that time ago. The ripples had ever since been coursing through their lives.

Len played the fiddle as the sun eased behind the mountain and the women served up the homemade peach ice cream and the children slumped damply against their mothers' legs, granny beads of mud ringing the creases of their necks. Len played the sad old ballads, until Wren called that this was a happy night and couldn't he pick it up a bit, and then Len ratcheted up the toe-tappers, and got the children so excited again that they danced in the grass.

The fireflies were out, and without Ruby knowing it, her brothers got up a Shiny Heinie night, and as they passed through the house on the way to their vehicles, they all released Mason jars of fireflies so that the rooms all began to glow with the little winged lamps.

Lucie ran from the kitchen to the dining room to the bedrooms, throwing her arms out and twirling in wonder. "The stars are inside," she cried. "The stars are inside."

So when Len and Lila started back up the mountain, where they had an RV set up, Lucie wanted to stay—if not so much to be with Something and Whatever, at least to sleep one night under the inside stars. Len and Lila kissed her good night and went out to their pickup. Ruby stood in the doorway and watched their headlights carve a tunnel of light into the dark trees rising up the mountain to Shoulderblade.

And then she turned into her own home and made a

bed for Lucie in the room just off theirs. The little girl was limp with exhaustion, and she crawled into bed without complaint as the fireflies flickered high in the corners of the room and along the iron headboard and even on her pillow.

"Sing something," she said drowsily. "Mama sings to me."

And so Ruby and Dewey sat on the rag rug by the bed, holding hands and singing the only song that came to mind, singing it soft and slow as a lullaby.

Lucie was asleep even before they got to the last stanza, but they sang on anyway, singing to each other and against all the time lost. *"Many a dark and stormy night. When I went home with you . . ."* Dewey touched Lucie's hair, and Ruby traced the outline of her little hand where it lay, fingers curled, on top of the quilt. By the light of the fireflies, Dewey looked at Ruby with everything he felt brimming in his eyes. And she leaned over and kissed him lightly on the temple, then on the top of his ear, where she paused to whisper the last little bit: *"I stumped my toe and down I go. Because I wanted you."*